DRAGON'S BLOOD

SPELLS FOR HIRE BOOK 4

STEFON MEARS

Also by Stefon Mears

Cavan Oltblood Series
Half a Wizard
The Ice Dagger
Spells of Undeath

Spells for Hire
Devil's Shoestring
Zombie Powder
Spirit Trap
Dragon's Blood

The Rise of Magic
Magician's Choice
Sleight of Mind
Lunar Alchemy
Three Fae Monte
The Sphinx Principle

The Telepath Trilogy
Surviving Telepathy
Immoral Telepathy
Targeting Telepathy

Edge of Humanity
Caught Between Monsters
Hunting Monsters

Power City Tales
Not Quite Bulletproof
No Money in Heroism

Devil's Night
Portal-Land, Oregon
Stealing from Pirates
Fade to Gold
With a Broken Sword
Twice Against the Dragon
The House on Cedar Street
Sudden Death
On the Edge of Faerie
Confronting Legends (Spells & Swords Vol. 1)
Uncle Stone Teeth and Other Macabre Poems
The Patreon Collection, Vol. 1-4 (Vol. 5, coming soon)

Published by Thousand Faces Publishing, Portland, Oregon

http://1kfaces.com

ISBN: 978-1-948490-31-3

Dragon's Blood

Spells for Hire | Book Four

AUTHOR'S NOTE

Spells for Hire stories take place in a world that is very like our own, but is not our own.

Thus, you might be able to visit some of the locations described in this story, such as Forest Park. Others, however, have been fictionalized or invented whole cloth. Where I have fictionalized or invented, I have tried to maintain that unique Portland vibe.

In much the same way, religions such as Vodou, Candomblé and Shugendō exist in this world, as do other practices such as Hoodoo. I have done substantial research in my attempts to keep my portrayals true to the spirit of those beliefs and practices. I have, however, taken liberties for dramatic purposes. I hope that devotees of those religions and practices will forgive any mistakes I have made.

PROLOGUE

THIS DAY HAD BEEN ON HEATH CYR'S CALENDAR FOR WEEKS.

His grandmother was flying into Portland to see him. All the way from New York. Nonstop, because Heath insisted on paying for the flight when she said she wanted to come. And Heath's beloved grandmother would never face a layover or plane-change if *he* had anything to say about it.

Hell, he'd've paid for first class if she wouldn't have given him *the look* for it.

He paid for business class anyway, because the woman was nearing seventy-five and shouldn't have to deal with coach on a six-hour flight.

No one should, really. But least of all Heath's grandmother.

Nana Cyr was due to touch down at PDX at two-thirty-seven p.m.

Her flight would be on time. Heath had no doubts about that. Heath himself was conjure man enough to ensure it, if he thought he needed to.

But Nana Cyr, she was a *manbo*. A Vodou priestess. Retired, mostly, but no less powerful for it.

Heath had no doubts that Papa Legba cleared the skies for her, all the way from New York to Oregon.

And when her plane landed, if Heath had a choice in the matter, he would be there to meet her. Preferably with some fresh chrysanthemums.

Better still to show up with his girlfriend, Nariko, by his side.

Heath might even have rented a suit for the occasion. Rented, because he knew she wouldn't approve of the only suit he bothered owning — the suit he'd bought because he knew she'd ask if he owned one, and if he didn't she'd hear the lie in his voice — and he sure as hell wasn't dropping the money on a new one he wouldn't wear again as soon as she left town.

Portland was a casual city. Heath liked that about it. Still, to pick up his grandmother, he would have worn a suit to make her happy.

Yes, if Heath had been able to arrange everything to his satisfaction, that was how he would have done it.

Unfortunately, none of those elements were coming together.

No way Nariko could be there.

She'd been out at Mount Hood for weeks — not that Heath would admit aloud where she was, even in private — for important reasons that dealt with her Shugendō practice, and, well, family problems.

She was due back today too, but Heath didn't know when.

Worse, Heath himself would not be able to meet Nana Cyr at the airport. Not after that phone call he got last night.

No, regardless of what Heath wanted, he would need his friend Colin to pick his grandmother up at the airport.

Colin. A very good friend, but he more than earned his nickname of Weird Colin. Yeah, most people only called him that because his magic was so strange.

Getting real, useful magic out of self-help books from the Seventies? Only Colin.

Heath wasn't worried about Colin's *magic* upsetting his grandmother. Colin's penchant for heavy metal tee shirts and ... distressed jeans, though. Not to mention his sense of humor, and the kind of questions he'd consider appropriate...

Yes, Heath fully expected he'd hear about those things later. But if Heath couldn't go himself — and he couldn't send Nariko — Colin was a solid option.

And unfortunately, Heath couldn't go himself.

Because Heath, he had someplace he simply had to be...

1

Heath Cyr arrived for his "business meeting" three hours early. Sipped a cup of good, strong black coffee, while sitting at an outdoor café across the street from the designated location.

The Set Piece Brewpub.

Two story brick place, with its own parking lot. Located at the corner of southwest 20th and Salmon, in a Portland neighborhood called Goose Hollow. Probably because it used to be run by gangs of geese or something like that.

Chichi little shopping district nowadays, near Portland's soccer stadium, Providence Park.

And given the huge signs supporting the Timbers and Thorns that filled the darkened pub windows, the management of the Set Piece Brewpub clearly loved their local soccer teams.

And here Heath had thought this was strictly a basketball town.

The Set Piece Brewpub was the last place Heath would have picked on his own to sit and have a meal. But then, he didn't follow sports. And nothing about this was his idea.

Heath had been "invited" to a "business" lunch by three other local practitioners.

Strange, that. Just not how things were done here, in the Portland occult community.

If those three had something to talk about, they should have met him at Gripper, *the* bar for such conversations. Bought him a drink and talked shop where the rules were clear, and everyone involved would know they were safe.

Starting trouble at Gripper was a recipe for great personal misfortune.

But these three didn't want to meet at Gripper. They wanted to buy Heath lunch. Someplace "out of the way."

Far as Heath was concerned, this might mean a declaration of war. With the opening salvo for dessert.

Most likely it didn't. Could even have been that they wanted his help with something that might have been embarrassing to talk about at Gripper.

Heath couldn't imagine what that might be, though. And the way the year had been going, it seemed more likely that he'd managed to piss off all three of them without even knowing he'd done it.

Still.

Heath never would have expected DeAndre McDaniels, a rival conjure man right here in town, to hire him for conjure work.

And yet, only days ago DeAndre had approached Heath in the café of Powell's City of Books and done just that.

DeAndre had had his reasons, and maybe these three did as well. Maybe.

Which meant Heath needed to take the meeting. Could be too good an opportunity to pass up.

And if they *did* intend an attack, well, Heath intended to be more than ready for them.

So Heath had foregone his usual love of sleeping in, much to the chagrin of his tuxedo cat, Dr. John.

Heath spent the morning preparing a number of small, wax envelopes filled with measures and charms he hoped he didn't need today.

He'd filled the pockets of his khaki cargo shorts with those envelopes, along with two conjure hands oriented around protection, and a few of the extras he always carried, just in case.

The most important options were in the pockets of his short-sleeved, button-up red-and-white striped shirt. Quick and easy access.

And, of course, anything else Heath was likely to need was waiting in his trademark black canvas backpack, which at the moment sat on the sidewalk, at Heath's feet.

Heath checked his phone. No updates about Nana Cyr, but in this case, no news was good news. No updates meant he could focus on what he was doing.

It was noon now. Two hours before the meeting.

Heath had spent the last hour just watching the foot traffic in the area. All of it looked innocent enough, and dressed for the mid-September heat.

Nice and casual, even for a lunch crowd, but that was Portland. Most of the suits would be down closer to the river.

That had taken some getting used to when Heath had first moved to Portland. He'd spent much of his youth in Manhattan, where suits were as common as trees were here.

In fact, Heath had wondered for a few months if there was an inverse relation between the number of trees in a city and the number of suits. He never went as far as trying to prove it though.

Nothing about the lunch crowd that day struck Heath as unusual.

The Set Piece Brewpub did pretty good traffic for a Friday morning, but nothing that set off any alarms in his head.

And by now Heath was sure he had the feel of the neighborhood, so it was time to take a more serious look around.

Most practitioners Heath knew, they'd start any surveillance with magic. Call up a spirit or two, or just open their spirit eyes — using whatever name they used for looking around with magical senses — and see what there was to see.

But Heath was a conjure man. Far as Heath was concerned, using actual magical senses would come about fifth in his personal order.

Heath wanted to get a good, strong feel of the weather on his skin, so he'd notice any changes. And today, that meant moderate heat, with enough humidity that it was likely to rain before the weekend ended.

Heath wanted to get the sounds of the neighborhood in his head. Not just the flow of passing car traffic or the conversations of the locals about their own business. He needed to know the sounds of the neighborhood itself.

Where and how often the loud air conditioners kicked on. What birds and insects kicked up a ruckus. That sort of thing.

Especially the insects and small animals. They were often the first to react to anything noteworthy.

In this case, construction was going on two blocks over. Hammering, sawing, plus a loud, regular *kerchunk* sound of some kind of heavy equipment.

No particular insect noises, apart from the occasional fly.

Birds in the neighborhood were mostly crows and meadowlarks, to judge by the songs. And birdsongs, those followed only insects and frogs on Heath's list of the most important things to notice.

All too many spirits liked to make bird noises.

Heath finished his coffee, scooped up his backpack and slung it over one shoulder.

He merged into the flow of foot traffic, and had to fight down the old Manhattan instinct to accelerate, using elbows as necessary.

Heath waited for the light before crossing, even though many around him did not.

When the light was with him, he crossed. Took a lap of the brewpub, nice and slow.

Three ways in. Double-doors at the corner. Glass. A kitchen door in the back. Wood. The third, a reinforced wooden door with two locks and a metal kick plate.

Windows along the sides facing Salmon and NW 20th. All darkened. No windows facing the parking lot.

Parking lot was full. No vehicles Heath had seen before. Just the usual mix of Subarus, hybrids and trucks that seemed to be the major choices for Portland area drivers.

A couple of the cars had bumper stickers with Wiccan pentacles and the like, but it was just tourist stuff. Or maybe the religious types, who worshiped their Goddess, but never sullied their hands with anything as dirty as magic.

Smart move on their part, if so.

Magic was a dangerous path. Not one Heath would recommend to anyone. Not anyone he liked, anyway.

Heath double-checked those cars for spells, all the same, and they came up clean.

Nothing along the perimeter of the brewpub to worry about.

Except maybe that reinforced door.

A cobweb up in the corner of it suggested that this door didn't open very often. Which meant it wasn't usually used by employees, much less the public.

Great place to sneak someone inside...

Heath dribbled a little of a special red dust along the door frame while muttering a short prayer to Papa Legba, who watched over all the ways in and out of places. If that door opened before sunset, Heath would know it.

Then it was time to go inside.

Backpack slung over one shoulder, Heath made his way back around to the front of the Set Piece Brewpub. The noontime rush kept the streets around him busy, but so far as Heath could tell, the traffic still looked innocent.

Innocent, in this case, meant that no one either avoided his gaze or watched him intently. Most people doing surveillance would do one or the other, when they should have been matching the friendly tone of Portland, where smiling and nodding at strangers was a common thing.

Even most professionals, on making eye contact with a target, would wonder for just a split-second if they'd been made. Oh, nothing would show on their face or in their posture, but reading people, that was just part and parcel to what Heath did.

On eye contact even with a pro, Heath would know.

Like after that Saint Cyprian business a few months back. The Lammergeyer sent a couple of Mob-types across the river from Vancouver to find out more about this Heath Cyr.

They were good. Took Heath the better part of an hour to spot them while he did some shopping at the Saturday Market.

He knew them the second he made eye contact.

After that, getting them to go away was a simple enough matter...

But Heath didn't have time to reminisce right now.

He pushed through the glass doors of the Set Piece Brewpub, and into the sounds of Irish folk music and the smell of good fried food.

Well, *decent* fried food. But Heath's standards for fried foods were pretty high.

He started craning to look back and forth, eyebrows down and a slight frown on his lips.

Couple of benches for people to sit on just inside the door, but no one waiting for a table right now.

Hostess was the blonde and bubbly type. Maybe five feet tall, so at least a foot shorter than Heath. Tanned, for a white girl in Portland, and wearing a green shirt that advertised an airline, of all things.

She started to speak, but Heath held up a hand to stall her, continuing to look around.

Bar proper was off to the right. Booths along the walls on all four sides. Four-top tables through the main part of the floor.

Three types of things covered the walls: flat screen televisions — all showing soccer games — news clippings about past championships, and Timbers and Thorns paraphernalia. The latter included things like signed photos and jerseys (apparently the airline ad was part of the Timbers jersey), and a ridiculous number of scarves.

High ceiling above the restaurant and bar, but not at the back. If the brewpub had a second story, it was only in the back half, which meant there were stairs back there somewhere.

Interesting. Private upstairs room for parties or clandestine meetings?

"Meeting somebody?" the hostess finally asked.

"Supposed to be," Heath said. "Don't see them yet. Mind if I use the restroom?"

"Be my guest," she said with a smile, and pointed it out. Back on the left hand side, near the kitchen.

Heath made his way over there, slowly. Double-checking the diners from the corners of his eyes while pretending to check out the décor.

No one paid him any special mind. One or two glances, but strictly innocent or flirtatious.

Past the restrooms, the hall had two doors into the kitchen, and two more interior doors toward the back, both labeled for employees only.

Hallway was a dead end. Neither of the two back doors he'd seen led into this hallway.

Two bathrooms in the place. Both unisex. One currently in use, so Heath entered the other.

Single room with no stalls. A urinal, a toilet, and a sink, along with an industrial-strength blow dryer in place of towels.

Room smelled like chemical disinfectant, and just a little urine. Either they cleaned it recently, or their patrons weren't so bad, for a place that served alcohol.

Heath hung his backpack on the coat hook, and dug through it for a blue bottle small enough to fit comfortably in his hand.

"All right," Heath whispered to the spirit inside the bottle. "Check the place out, especially the kitchen and bar. You find a *trace* of anything out of the ordinary, you tell me."

The spirit that came out of the bottle belonged to a witch who preferred being called Morgana over the name on her birth certificate. Morgana had lived and died out in the Portland suburb of Hillsboro, and wasn't happy about how the latter was handled.

She'd haunted her family because they hadn't done right by her remains. They'd buried her, when she'd stated plainly in her will that she wanted to become compost, feeding a tree. Even set aside money to make it happen.

After Heath straightened that mess out, Morgana had agreed to work with Heath for a time, so long as he fed her weekly wafts of dragon's blood incense.

Morgana's spirit eyes had been pretty impressive when she was alive. And now that she was dead, her vision was even better. If there were any traps waiting, she'd find them.

While Heath waited, he checked himself in the mirror. Could have shaved a little closer, but his brown curls looked good. And his skin tone was dark enough that no one was likely to notice the little stubble he'd missed, not until evening.

Morgana gave the all-clear when she came back in, and zoomed right back into her bottle.

Morgana had proven she wouldn't lie to him. And Heath had no reason to doubt her skills.

Still. All clear.

Heath didn't trust that for a moment.

After leaving the restroom and making his apologies to the bubbly hostess, Heath retreated back across the street to his vantage point at the outdoor café.

There Heath sipped at coffee, waited, and watched.

Two hours passed under the early afternoon clouds without the world ending, anyone trying to kill him, or even anyone trying to sneak spells onto the Set Piece Brewpub.

An encouraging start to the day, all things considered.

Heath watched as they arrived, these three practitioners who had "invited" Heath to this "business lunch."

Tommy Wong arrived first. Expensive black suit over a trim physique. Dark blue tie. Little yin-yang tie tack. The kind of haircut where his black hairs were cut short, but stood up on top of his head. As Tommy Wong entered the Set Point Brewpub, Heath estimated the man stood just a couple of inches shorter than Heath himself.

Taoist sorcerer and alchemist, Tommy Wong. Looked like he

might be in his mid-twenties, like Heath, but he might have been hundreds of years old, for all Heath knew.

Taoist sorcerers had the reputation for living very, very long lives.

Peaceful expression on his face. As though Tommy Wong didn't have a care in the world.

Celia Martinez followed a minute or two later. Somewhere in middle age, Celia Martinez, with as much gray as black in the hair piled on top of her head. Red and yellow dress over a heavy frame, but she carried her weight well.

Curandera, Celia Martinez. Which made her a root worker in her own right. Not quite the same kind of practitioner as Heath, but her style was more closely related to Heath's than either of the other two who would be present for today's "meeting."

Celia Martinez looked eager, but that could have meant anything.

Stetson Price arrived last. Young enough to be a college student, he was a big white boy in every sense. Even taller than Heath, and broad from both muscle and fat. He had short, curly black hair and an equally curly black beard. Wore jeans and sneakers, along with some kind of gray tee shirt, though Heath couldn't see the decoration on the front. Not from where he sat.

Witch, Stetson Price. Some kind of family tradition that had been in Portland for some fifty years, but went all the way back to the "Old World." By reputation, calling him a Wiccan or a warlock would be an insult worthy of a challenge.

His family were witches, and proud of it.

Stetson Price was whistling when he arrived. Looked excited.

Heath let them all wait a minute or two before he made his way over to join them at the Set Piece Brewpub.

As Heath crossed the street from his stakeout spot at the outdoor café, he tested the feel of the atmosphere against the benchmarks he'd already established.

The day — still warm and just a little humid.

The birds — still crows and meadowlarks, and still acting normal. No odd changes to their behavior.

The insects — still pretty much just the occasional fly.

Foot traffic ... car traffic ... the sounds of nearby construction ... all consistent with what Heath would expect.

All of that was good news. No changes to any of these things, meant no new spells had been added between here and there.

True. The three of them might have done something inside, but Heath would know one way or the other soon enough.

He pushed through those glass doors and once more into the smells of fried foods and the sounds of Irish folk music.

A quick stretch of his feelings and glance through his spirit eyes told Heath that there'd been no changes inside either.

So far, so good.

The bubbly blonde hostess greeted Heath like an old friend.

"On time now?" she asked with a smile that could have been blinding under naked sunlight.

"Hope so," Heath said, faking an embarrassed smile. He'd already spotted the other three sitting at a booth in the left-hand corner, under the window, but he pretended he didn't. "I'm looking for—"

"Over here!"

That Stetson Price had a booming voice. Cut right across the music, the clattering of dishware and the background conversations.

"Twilight!" the big man called, in case missed his first shout.

Heath fought down a sigh. He'd been handed that nickname not long after he'd moved to Portland, and it had stuck.

Heath was the kind of guy who lived on the edges of a lot of things. Black and white magic. His mother's pale Irish skin and his father's blue-black African heritage. "Twilight" seemed to encompass them all, and a few other things besides.

But if he had to answer one more damned question about vampires...

"Let me guess," the hostess said, still smiling as she pointed. "That's your group?"

"Lucky me," Heath said through a forced smile, and made his way to their booth.

A booth, not a table. Two sides, not four. Either they wanted to make sure that Heath stayed in easy arm's reach, or they wanted a pretense of confederation.

Someone would be sitting on Heath's side, after all, instead of each on his or her own side.

Maybe.

Or maybe the hostess led them to a booth and no one questioned it.

Too hard to tell, at this point.

They'd left Heath a seat beside Stetson Price, with the other two facing him. All three of them were smiling.

Heath set his backpack down between his feet as he sat.

"So," he said, while the waiter brought them water, "why are we here and not at Gripper?"

"Don't tell me you don't like this place," Stetson said, sounding scandalized.

"Perhaps he is not fond of football," Tommy said. "Or supports another team."

Then Celia must have read something in Heath's posture, or maybe his expression. Or maybe she just noticed the he tried to watch all three of them at the same time.

"It's not that at all," she said quickly. She reached into the neckline of her dress and pulled out a worn, old wooden crucifix, on a leather thong that looked just as old and worn.

She pulled the crucifix up over her head, kissed it, and set it on the table in front of Heath.

"This has been in my family for generations," she said, giving Heath intense eye contact, with her honey dark eyes. "My great, great grandmother received it from the hand of Pope Leo XIII."

Heath nodded, eyes narrowed. The crucifix did feel old enough for that to be true. To know more he'd have to look with his spirit eyes, but that might draw attention, with all three watching him.

"It has been handed down to firstborn daughters in my family,"

Celia continued, while still looking Heath in the eye, "whenever the current holder retires from healing work."

She slid the crucifix toward him. Allowed Heath to move it out of anyone's reach but his.

Celia crossed herself and spoke an oath.

"I solemnly swear in the name of the Father that our intentions here today are peaceful, and that not one of the three of us means you a threat. If, at any point before we leave here, you believe I have lied to you about this, or feel that any of us threatens or acts against you, I bid you to take this crucifix and use it against me as you will."

Heath whistled. He had seen the offering-a-link approach done before, most recently by DeAndre McDaniels.

But this...

This was probably just about the strongest link Celia Martinez could have offered. No way she could have been anything but perfectly serious, and entirely confident in the other two.

Celia Martinez wasn't just handing Heath a loaded gun. She was willingly sitting under a sixteen ton weight, and giving Heath the handle that would drop it.

"Oh, *Aradia*," Stetson said, his jaw dropping in shock. Perhaps a little slow to understanding. "You thought—"

"He thought he was being invited here," Tommy said in even tones, "to be threatened, challenged, or attacked. I do apologize. I mean nothing of the sort, nor do either of these others."

"I'll confirm that," Stetson said. "Don't have a link that good to offer you, but—"

Stetson stopped talking as the waiter returned for drink orders. The other three ordered both drinks and food without consulting the menu, as though they ate here all the time.

Heath, though he definitely felt more relaxed about the meeting, wasn't willing to relax all the way. He ordered tacos — something he ordered only rarely and only from certain food carts, so they could not have been ready for him to order them — and a bottle of Newcastle Brown Ale. A decent beer, but again, not one of his regular brands.

Still, Heath knew the smell of that beer well. It was one of four brands whose smells and tastes he'd learned specifically for instances like this one.

If anything were slipped into his bottle, he was confident he could tell.

Yeah, he was pretty sure they were serious. But they might have had allies not at the table and thus, not bound by their words.

Not to mention that some people didn't consider magical *influence* in the same category as magical *attack*...

"All right," Heath said when the waiter was gone. "So you've told me what we're *not* doing here. If this really is business, what do you want to hire me to do?"

"Hire you?" Stetson asked, sounding confused.

"May I?" Tommy asked the other two, but it was Heath that answered.

"I'd say that Celia here has paid for the right to speak first."

That got Heath a warm smile from Celia.

"Heath," she said thoughtfully, "how many times have you been drawn into conflicts with other practitioners since you moved here?"

Loaded question. Even counting only the past year and a half, Heath had lost a very public fight with another rootworker named *Vizinha,* though he'd beaten her soundly the more recent time they tangled. A western ceremonial magician called Drake had also challenged Heath to a duel to the death in front of the entire community, at Gripper. A duel Heath had managed to win without killing the idiot.

And those were just the big conflicts that leapt right to mind. If he started counting the smaller ones...

"Oh, I've had my share," Heath said with a one-shoulder shrug. "Maybe a little more. Why?"

"That's a sad statement," she said. "That you *expect* conflicts with other practitioners."

"Well," Heath said, then waited while the drinks arrived.

Heath studied the neck of his sweating bottle of Newcastle Brown. Sniffed it.

Safe.

"Those of us who choose to sell spells," Heath continued after a tasty swig, "we're bound to squabble from time to time. Over clients, territory and so on."

"What if you didn't have to?" Tommy Wong asked in a smooth, even tone.

"What if," Stetson said, leaning forward and not hiding the excitement in his tone, "what if there was an alternative means of resolving conflicts?"

"If you're trying to sell me Tupperware, I'm not interested," Heath said through a sigh. "And I'm pretty sure no one needs encyclopedia on their bookshelves anymore. So whatever you're selling, get to the point."

Celia held up a hand to the other two, taking lead back.

"The Portland metro area," Celia said, "is one of the most populous regions of the United States without some form of council, leadership, or oversight among its community of practitioners."

"Why do you think I moved here?" Heath asked, chuckling.

That stopped the three of them. Stetson's mouth even hung open in surprise.

Heath smiled and shook his head.

"Funny thing happens when you start giving people authority. They start to like it. They start to abuse it. In little ways, at first, maybe. Help themselves. Help their friends. Feel entitled, because of the work they're putting in. Next thing you know you're getting *laws*. Edicts. Constraints punishable by their enforcement arm, using links you were required to hand over."

Heath stopped smiling and shook his head again.

"Fuck. That."

"Where in the United States," Tommy asked, "is anyone required to hand over links to an enforcement body?"

"That I haven't heard of it happening yet doesn't mean it hasn't or won't," Heath said, setting down his beer. "Besides. Whether an abuse is big or small, it's still an abuse of power. And if I consent to be governed, then it's power over *me* being abused, and my own fault for letting it happen."

"Authority does not guarantee corruption," Tommy said.

Heath smiled nice and wide.

"Look at our governments and say that again," Heath said. He pointed at each of the three in turn. "You're either Chinese or of Chinese descent, Tommy. The rumors conflict on that point. Going to tell me China has no corruption?"

Before Tommy could answer, Heath turned to Celia. "Second generation Mexican American, I believe. Same question about Mexico."

Again, Heath didn't wait for a reply before turning to Stetson. "And Stetson, your family's been here for umpteen generations or something. Don't you *dare* have the balls to tell me the United States doesn't have corruption or abuse of power. The examples are a list that would take weeks to compile, and even then only scratch the surface."

"What if you were part of this council?" Celia interrupted, when Stetson looked as though he were going to try a comeback. "You could help prevent corruption from taking root."

"Just means I'd end up being the most corrupt of all." Heath shook his head. "People do the worst things with the best of intentions."

"If you do not trust yourself with power," Tommy asked, more curiosity in his voice than anything else, "why did you take up the path of sorcery?"

"Didn't choose it," Heath said. "Let's just say it chose me."

No way Heath was telling these people how his own uncle tried to offer his soul to a Lwa, Baron Samedi, in exchange for power. Nor how it was another Lwa, Papa Legba, who saved Heath.

Heath took up the path of conjure out of self-defense.

Still, they were paying for lunch. So Heath was polite enough to listen to their arguments. Though he did offer refutations at every turn.

And he made sure to order a big slice of chocolate cake for dessert.

If he had to put up with this kind of sales pitch for his meal — not to mention letting someone else pick his grandmother up at the airport — he was going to get as much out of that meal as he could.

AT LEAST THE "MEETING" DIDN'T RUN ALL AFTERNOON, THE WAY HEATH had feared it might. Didn't take much more than an hour for Tommy Wong, Celia Martinez and Stetson Price to admit to themselves that they'd been barking up the wrong tree.

Heath didn't support any kind of "central organization" to the occult community of Portland, and he sure as hell didn't want to be part of one.

Still, they'd been affable enough about it. Didn't hesitate about paying the check. Even left all smiles, like this had been some kind of a productive meeting instead of a colossal waste of everyone's time.

Heath found that kind of suspicious, but figured they were just trying to save face. People could be like that.

Still, that Stetson Price, he didn't seem the type to hide his emotions too well. And even he seemed to take Heath's rejection pretty well. Even if he seemed convinced that Heath would come around, "once he understood what was at stake."

"What was at stake..."

Those words, this time, were spoken by a priest. Or a monk. Or a monk-priest. Heath was never quite sure where to put the emphasis when he thought about Brother Tony of the Protective Order of Saint Benedict.

But one thing was for sure about Tony — he dressed the part, regardless of the weather or circumstances.

All black wool, ankle to neck, worn over a build like a wrestler — Greco-Roman, to go with his nose. None of those little priest collars for him, but no one could possibly have mistaken Tony for anything other than what he was.

Even here, back at Heath's table at that little outdoor café across the street from the Set Point Brewpub, the late-summer heat and touch of humidity didn't seem to bother Tony in the slightest.

Normally, Heath would never have gone back to a surveillance spot right after the meeting like this, except for two things.

One, he was sure those three were gone. Tony had been keeping watch, and confirmed it.

And two, the coffee really was worth coming back for.

"His words exactly," Heath confirmed, sipping his cup of rich coffee. "Once I understood what was at stake."

"Any sense of what he meant by it?" Tony asked, sipping from his own cup of coffee loaded with milk.

Heath shook his head. "That Stetson Price, he doesn't seem to be the sharpest knife in the block, if you take my meaning. I'm not too sure he meant anything more complicated than that eventually I'd come around to his way of thinking."

"Except..." Tony said, giving Heath a big dose of those demanding black eyes of his. Tony's Italian heritage always seemed to show most in the tone of his skin and the color of his eyes.

In Heath's opinion, anyway.

"Except that," Heath said with a shrug, "if *I* were somebody like Tommy Wong or Celia Martinez, and I wanted to leave a line like that on somebody like *me*, I'd feed it to Stetson before the meeting. That way Stetson says the words, but the mark doesn't take it as a threat the way he would from Celia or Tommy."

"Mark?" Tony raised one eyebrow, but Heath wasn't sure if that was amusement or concern. The two looked the same on Tony sometimes.

Heath shrugged again. "I still think they were trying to play me a bit, but that might just be my suspicious nature."

"Or they have something planned," Tony said, "and they're trying to figure out how you'll respond."

"There is that," Heath confirmed with a nod. "The question then is why bring this to me."

"You do get yourself into some interesting positions."

"Yeah, well," Heath said and checked his phone. No updates yet. "I'd rather have gotten myself into that position yesterday and been at the airport today."

"You could have let *me* pick her up," Tony said, showing the kind of insight Heath would expect from a good priest.

Heath chuckled.

"Oh, I doubt Colin's going to get me into *that* much trouble. Besides. If I'd sent a priest ... or a monk ... to pick her up, might send the wrong message."

"What?" Tony asked as though he could possibly make the question sound innocent. "That you might be returning to the fold?"

"Not happening," Heath said firmly. "I like my Unitarian freedom, thank you very much."

"Too late for that," Tony teased. "Once you're baptized, you're ours. No take-backs."

"But—"

"And I *believe* you've been confirmed?" Tony asked over the rim of his coffee cup.

"You know damn well I only did that for my parents. I don't like the way the Church—"

"Doesn't matter," Tony said, smiling as though he'd just outmaneuvered Heath on a chessboard. Not that Heath would play chess with Tony. He just seemed the type. "Any chance you had of escaping us fled with your catechism. You're ours, whether you say so or not."

"Yeah, well, tell it to the Lwa," Heath grumbled, and sipped his coffee again. The taste was still as rich and full, but it wasn't as pleasing as it had been a moment ago.

Heath had been told something very similar by two of the Lwa, the divine intermediaries of Vodou. Or was it three now? Papa Legba had definitely said it. And Ghede Brav had said it as well...

"Don't have to," Tony said, his smile widening. "Being a *Vodousiant* doesn't make you less Catholic. In fact, I think most *houngans* and *manbos* would say it—"

"Would say that's part of it, and I'm not saying I'm theirs either." Heath shook his head. "Can we get back to the topic?"

"You have a more important topic than your soul?"

"Right now I'm more concerned about that 'what's at stake' crack. Those three must have something in mind intended to show me — and maybe anyone else they've talked to who disagrees with them — that they're right. Some kind of plan..."

"So divine it," Tony said with a shrug.

"Never that easy," Heath said. "Even if Tommy and Stetson wouldn't think to obfuscate, Celia would. She knows I'd likely throw the cowries about this."

"If you're that concerned, I doubt they could cloud the Sybil's sight."

The Sybil of Portland. Far as Heath could tell, no one really knew who the Sybil was, or what her motivations were. But sometimes she just showed up at this one park in the west side business district, dressed as a street statue performer. Her look was that of a stage magician with a top hat and wand, painted silver head to toe.

And when she was present, she would look into the future for those who made the right kind of offering. Her predictions were unfailingly accurate, and unfailingly confusing.

Going to the Sybil would always get answers. And while those answers always proved accurate in retrospect, they weren't always useful in the moment...

Heath shook his head.

"Then what's the next move?"

Heath's phone buzzed.

"Finally," Heath said, answering the call from Colin.

"So," said a voice that wasn't Colin's, but Heath knew it all too well just the same. "What's so important that my grandson can't pick me up at the airport?"

Heath's grandmother had about three main tones of voice that Heath knew and knew well, and about six variations of each.

This tone was irritated, but reserving judgment before descending into *cross*.

And Heath did *not* want to make her cross.

"Well, Nana," Heath started, then realized that he even sounded guilty in his own ears. Just hearing that tone from her had made him feel sixteen again and caught out after curfew.

He sucked in a deep breath and tried again, while Tony smiled like he was holding back a laugh.

That, more than anything else, steadied Heath's nerves while he explained where he was, why he was there, and what his day had been like in enough detail that Tony's eyebrows were threatening his hairline by the time Heath was done.

Of course, Tony's surprise might also have been about being included in the recitation. How Tony had taken up Heath's surveillance spot as soon as Heath went inside for the meeting, and kept an eye on things from the outside.

By the time Heath finished, his mouth was dry, but he couldn't bring himself to sip any more of his cooling coffee.

He had more nerves jangling through his belly right then than he'd had at any point around that "business meeting."

"Well," Nana Cyr said in her *considering* voice, then finally finished with, "All right then. Sounds like you handled yourself well enough. But I expect you to get your butt home before your friend Colin gets me there."

Tony shot a look at Tony that must have shown every nerve he felt, because Tony set his cup down and said, "Let's go," without so much as a pleading word from Heath.

The last thing Nana Cyr said before Heath got off the phone with her was, "Your friend Colin ... is an *interesting* boy."

Maybe Heath should have let Tony pick her up after all.

HEATH DROPPED ENOUGH CASH TO DOUBLE THE BILL ON THE CAFÉ TABLE — as he'd done earlier — because this café had done well by Heath, and he wanted to show appreciation, even when he couldn't take the time to go through the normal bill-paying process.

From the sound of things, Nana Cyr was not in a mood to be kept waiting.

"I'm parked about a block over," Tony said, standing and turning straight for a side street. "This way."

"Wait," Heath said, standing stock still, backpack over one shoulder.

Tony, already four steps away, turned back, frowning, but Heath stilled the monk's questions with a raised hand.

Something was wrong.

While Tony stepped closer, Heath tried to determine what.

The mid-September warmth was the same. The humidity too. The crunching noise of the construction had stopped while Heath had been in the brewpub, but that fact hadn't portended anything. Either they'd finished with their big toy, or they'd finished for the day.

Traffic — both sidewalk and street — had eased up since the noon rush, but steadily. Nothing there to...

The birds.

The birds had gone quiet.

The meadowlarks might have moved on for the afternoon. Maybe over to Forest Park, walking distance from here. Easily inside whatever their normal daily range was.

But the crows? Uh uh.

They were still hereabouts. Heath could see a small murder of them in a baby elm tree halfway down the block to his left. North from where he stood. A couple of individuals flying overhead. Southeast to northwest...

The crows in the elm all took to the sky, cawing cawing cawing.

Somewhere up the street that direction a car backfired.

On the café table beside Heath, his coffee cup exploded into fragments.

That was no car backfiring.

Heath dove for concrete, close to a parked Subaru WRX. All the freaking SUVs around here and he had to be standing near a sedan?

"Gun!" Tony yelled in that same moment, joining Heath behind the car.

Tony's yell had about the effect Heath expected: panic.

People started screaming. Most of the ones on the street around him started running one direction or another.

Better if they'd found cover, but at least they were moving. Gave their adrenaline something to do.

Heath's own adrenaline had kicked up, of course. His mouth was dry and his heart was beating so fast and loud, if it were a bass drum, no team of Mardi Gras musicians could have kept up with it.

But his wits stayed right where they needed to be — in the moment.

In the street, a big four-by-four and one of the eco-friendly versions of an SUV slammed into each other in their haste to get away from the kill zone.

Another gunshot. This one hit the WRX. Another quick shot followed and took a chunk out of the sidewalk nearby.

Heath was starting to take this personally.

Worse, there was a woman with a kid, just standing there. Wealthy types, from the style of their summer clothes and haircuts. The kind of blonde and blessed folks that this sort of thing simply did not happen to.

Standing close enough another sidewalk shot might hit them.

They'd just come out of the candy store next door to the outdoor café and froze in place, holding each other. Little boy crying, and his mother staring, eyes so wide is was a wonder her eyeballs didn't fall out and bounce away down the street.

People tended to react to threats in one of three ways: run towards the danger, run away from the danger, or freeze.

The types who ran toward the danger tended to become first-responders, Navy SEALs, that kind of thing.

The types who ran from the danger tended to live the longest of the three.

The types who froze, well, they might not move until it was too late.

And Heath was looking at two freezers, standing only maybe five feet from where he and Tony were hiding.

Way too close to that last shot.

Damn it.

"Move to the next car," Heath said to Tony, pointing to a parked Prius maybe ten feet farther south along the street.

"Let me—"

Another gunshot slammed into the body of the WRX.

"Go!"

Heath didn't wait for a response.

He jumped from behind the car, just ahead of a bullet that took concrete from between his feet.

That one was too close.

Huh. Turned out Heath's heart *could* beat faster.

He didn't waste time on subtlety. He grabbed the woman and boy in his arms and half-carried them into that candy shop, accompanied by the shop's door chimes playing a few notes of "The Candy Man."

The smells of sugar, caramel and chocolate hit Heath's nose hard enough to make his stomach rumble, despite itself. Got a little saliva flowing into his dry mouth too, which was a blessing.

A bullet blew a hole in the candy store's plate glass window, but the window itself held. The tile floor behind it was not so lucky.

The store had little clear plastic bins of candy all over the walls, and a counter near the front where the employees were huddled.

Ah, they had the store safe between themselves and the street. Smart.

"There," Heath said, gently but firmly pushing the woman toward the employees. "Get down there and stay there until it's safe."

"What..." the woman started to say, but Heath didn't wait for her to finish. He just added a *listen-to-me* tone to his voice and tried again.

"Get down there with your boy and stay there until it's safe."

She nodded and helped her crying child down behind the counter and safe. Heath wasn't even sure the store's workers had noticed them until he'd said those last words.

But that was the blessing and the curse of the *listen-to-me* tone. It wasn't a true compulsion like the *compelling gaze*, but it cut through all the bullshit in the listener's head and made them hear his words.

Of course, it also made sure everybody *nearby* heard his words too.

Now Heath had to worry about whether or not the store clerks would let strangers hide with them.

Two clerks. A middle-aged, middle-eastern man with a salt-and-pepper hair and a heavy mustache, and a teenage boy with a tight fade and skin darker than Heath's, who looked more like a football player than a candy salesman despite the brightly colored uniform.

Both stared at Heath, wide-eyed with fear. For a moment, Heath thought he'd need to say something, but then the man shook himself and nodded at Heath.

The man quickly made sure the woman and boy had the safest spot. He gave the boy a lollipop, for something to focus on, and spoke reassuring words.

The boy even took a position that was still behind the safe, but if any threat came into the shop, he'd be there to meet it first.

Silence.

Not true silence, of course. The man was still talking softly, and there was still too much panic in the street. Not to mention the sound of approaching police sirens.

And, of course, Heath's heart still pounding as though trying to get his attention.

But of the sound that mattered most — gunshots — only silence.

Not more than five seconds or so, true, but it was the longest stretch so far.

Gunman could have been waiting for Heath to show his face again. Could have taken off.

And Heath had no doubt by now that he was the target. The shots were consistently too close, and without Heath's precautions, any one or all of them might have hit him.

"Well, Papa Legba," Heath muttered, "I hope you're watching over this little fool, because he needs to get home in one piece."

Heath pulled a packet blend of grains of paradise, poppy and red pepper. He kissed the packet, whispered a spin off of a Proverb, "Hey, Mr. Wicked, here's your troubled fountain and corrupt spring."

Heath blew the powder out the bullet hole in the plate glass window. Sent it out toward the gunman along the same path the bullet came in.

No, it wasn't as though the powder would physically reach the gunman. Didn't have to, to do its job. It was the angle that mattered. The symmetry.

A neat little confusion charm, if Heath said so himself. Of course, the gunman might have counter-charms, if he'd really been sent after Heath.

But Heath couldn't just sit and wait in this store all day.

"No!" The woman called from behind him as he started for the door. "Wait for the police!"

Heath appreciated the thought, but waiting for police was never high on his list of things to do. In fact, it was just another reason to get his butt in gear.

He closed his eyes and stepped back out onto the street.

No immediate gunfire. Good.

All the same, Heath hustled back to the cover of the WRX.

No one tried to kill him.

"Heath," Tony stage whispered from his spot by the Prius. "I tried to distract the gunman, but he—"

"He was targeting me," Heath said. "Think he's gone now. Let's get out of here."

"But the police..." Tony's words died as he saw the droll look on Heath's face.

"You really need me to explain it, I'll explain on the way."

Tony frowned like maybe he understood, when he thought about it a moment. He nodded and led the way to his car.

Tony was a priest, and a white boy. No doubt he could face an army of cops and be just fine, no matter what the situation.

But Heath? He could hear the conversation now.

You were standing where? Cops then looked at the shot pattern. Concluded Heath was the target, and promptly threw all presumption of innocence right out the window.

Then they would find out he was carrying a backpack full of

herbs, incenses and other "weird" things, and Heath would waste the day in a cell until a lab confirmed that everything on his person was legal.

Oh, and they'd have more questions for him, as long as he was there, because *of course* they'd assume he'd know why he was targeted...

Yeah. Even if his grandmother wasn't waiting, that didn't sound like Heath's kind of party.

2

———————

THE DRIVE FROM TONY'S PARKING SPOT TO HEATH'S PLACE ONLY TOOK about five minutes. All narrow side streets in the maze of northwest Portland.

Tony didn't say anything on the drive, for which Heath was grateful. He didn't need to talk right now. Heath just ... he needed a moment.

In fact, despite his rush, he wouldn't have minded if the drive home were longer. Might have given him a little longer to calm down. Get presentable before he saw his grandmother.

As it stood, even now his heart was still pounding, and he was shaking. Why was he shaking?

Had to have been adrenaline. Couldn't have been nerves.

Could it?

Someone had tried to shoot him. Someone had actually taken a rifle of some kind — at least Heath assumed the would-be assassin was packing more than a sidearm — and fired bullets at Heath on a city street. In Portland freaking Oregon. In broad daylight. With presumably lethal intent.

What. The. Hell.

Heath had dealt with plenty of people trying to kill him, but they'd pretty much always had the decency to play by the rules. Do the dirty work themselves, with whatever magic they brought to the table.

This, though. This was different. And different was concerning.

Who would try to kill him with a firearm? Or ... hire someone to do it?

Heath's mind raced back over the clients he'd worked with in the last several months. No unsatisfied customers.

Enemy of one of those customers, maybe? Trying to eliminate a source of aid?

Heath had helped three different women get rid of stalkery guys. Could one of those guys...

Heath shook his head. Sitting here in a car was no way to *logic* through an unknown. He needed information. He needed to do some homework.

Why did this have to happen *today*?

At least his grandmother wasn't here yet.

Heath was sure of that much, because he didn't see Colin's white Saturn parked on the street as Tony's immaculate old Subaru Forester rolled to a stop along the curb.

So at least *that much* had gone right today.

Then again, since no one seemed to be actively trying to kill him at the moment, maybe things were looking up.

A lovely thought, but not one he could trust...

"Hey," Tony said softly, handing Heath a sweating bottle of water. "Sip. Your throat's probably dry. If you feel too shaky to sip, put it against the back of your neck."

Heath drew breath to say something, but he must have had an objection all over his face because Tony pushed the bottle on him and spoke louder.

"You don't need to play tough right now. I can tell you've never been shot at before. You're dealing with at least some level of shock." The big monk frowned. "How much I can't quite tell with you. But that's all right. What you need to remember is that you aren't being shot at *now*. The immediate danger has passed."

"I—" Heath cleared his throat. "I know *that* much. But I—"

"No," Tony said, shaking his head. "You don't need answers *this second*. This second, you need to breathe. You need to center. And you need to sip a little of that water."

Heath frowned, but he uncapped the water bottle and sipped. Tasted better than he thought. No label on the bottle either, and it wasn't flimsy enough to be store bought...

"We bottle our own," Tony said through a smile, "from a well on the monastery grounds. Which is why I'll want the bottle back, when you're done. Waste not, want not."

Heath couldn't stop himself from chuckling. The water was too much on top of everything else.

He was sitting here in a powder blue Subaru Forester. The car was more than a decade old, but in absolutely flawless condition. Not so much as a spot or a sign of wear on the gray cloth seats or matching interior. Might have come straight from a museum, if not for the scent of frankincense.

He was talking to a guy who looked like he should have been an extra in a mob movie. The hitman disguised as a priest. Right down to his nose, which had been broken at least once.

And *this* was the man telling him how to handle being shot at. Discussing it so casually you'd think he'd spent a decade as a Green Beret or something. Or maybe *had been* that mob hitter.

And now he was worried about the future of a single plastic bottle.

That was just too much.

Heath's chuckle turned into a laugh. And before he knew it, Tony was laughing right along with him.

"Good," Tony said. "Laughter's good. As long as it doesn't get hysterical."

Heath let the laugh peter out. Met Tony's eyes. Realized he wasn't shaking anymore. His heartbeat was back to a normal rate too.

Heath nodded. Tony nodded back, a satisfied look in his eyes.

"Good," Tony said. "You want to talk about this later, I'm here."

Heath nodded again, and got out of the car, stepping out onto the curb.

Heath's neighborhood was quiet right now, but that was normal. He lived in a pretty quiet neck of the woods. Almost literally.

Heath's place was tucked away in one of the little neighborhoods near the aptly named Forest Park.

And it definitely was *aptly named*. During Heath's youth in Manhattan, he'd thought Central Park was pretty big. Not as big as some of the places he'd seen outside of New Orleans as a kid, but for a city? Huge.

Forest Park dwarfed Central Park.

More than five thousand acres of *actual* forest, pretty much all of which was within Portland city limits.

Urban forest, for a city that always seemed at least half-forest to Heath anyway. Conveniently close to Heath's home as both a source of free-growing herbs and supplies, as well as tucked away spots of nature for certain kinds of workings.

The block around Heath's place had mostly cute little one and two bedroom houses struggling for space. But every so often, you could spot a home that was decades old and had never sold off any of its land.

Heath lived in a place like that.

Not the great big house in front. That had been split into four apartments, currently full of about ten college kids, living in town to study over at PSU.

At least, that was what Heath had gathered from conversations he'd had with a few of the new tenants while he collected recent mail.

Only a couple of years younger than Heath himself, but they were all so ... perky. The guys and the girls. Like life was the best thing they could imagine, and every day got better than the one before it.

Every so often, Heath wondered what it would feel like to live life that way.

'Course, knowing the things Heath knew, if he tried that attitude it would get him killed.

He never would have been ready for someone taking pot shots at him...

So, quiet for Heath's neighborhood meant that he could hear lawnmowers running somewhere in the next block or so, and the distant honking and revving of traffic, and the faint strains of some woman pop singer coming from the house in front.

Otherwise, just the breeze, and the kind of standard birdsongs and squirrel chatter that Heath was used to.

Further, the couple of spirits that Heath had keeping an eye on his place didn't act like anything unexpected was happening. That was definitely a good thing. The wards were all up and running too without a hint that anything had tried to get through. Even better.

Never a good thing, to come home to damaged wards.

Heath's apartment was around back. A little standalone building, tucked in among a small grove of Douglas fir trees, and a solid variety of Oregon native plants.

The rhododendrons and roses were looking pretty good. Gardeners must have been doing their jobs all right. The Oregon grapes and ferns could both use a little more rain, but that would come along soon enough.

Did they look good enough for Nana Cyr?

No. But better she have those to complain about outside. Maybe she'd look a little less for something to complain about *in*side.

As though Heath would be so lucky.

At least the ground cover looked good. Three varieties of mint did the job, surrounding the little walkway to Heath's porch, and the stepping stone walking path that meandered through the backyard. For those who wanted a walk, but were too lazy for a hike over at Forest Park.

Heath was just about to turn his attention to his own house when a little spirit popped up in front of him. Looked kind of like a cartoon fairy, if that cartoon were drawn for some porno rag. Ridiculous proportions under gauzy silk, and wispy blond hair.

One of Colin's artificial spirits. Heath didn't even need to look hard at it to know that much. Only Colin would send him a messenger that looked like this one.

Tony frowned at Heath's abrupt stop, but his eyes weren't fixed on the right spot. Maybe he couldn't see the messenger?

Interesting.

"Heath," the messenger said in a breathy voice, "Colin and your grandmother are pulling up to the curb now."

"Thank you," Heath said, bowing from the neck, "and unless there's more to your message, you better scat. My gran will *not* want to see you."

She flitted away.

"Word from Colin?" Tony said.

Heath nodded, and drew a deep breath. He turned to face the street. Saw Colin's Saturn pull up at the curb next door.

"My grandmother's here."

As Heath hustled back to the front of the property, Tony following about a step behind, he tried to remember the state he'd left his apartment in.

Normally, he was a pretty clean worker, whether he was cooking or conjuring. But with thoughts of the business meeting and the potential for attacks — without even *considering* the possibility of a gunman — not to mention doing all that prep work hours before he even should have been awake...

Well, he'd just have to hope he'd cleaned up after himself.

Heath made it back to the front of the house and all the way to the passenger side door before his grandmother could open it.

An accomplishment in and of itself. His grandmother didn't mind having doors opened for her, but she was never of a mind to sit and *wait* for a door to open either.

Colin was already out of the car and opening the trunk.

At least he'd dressed up a *little* for the occasion. His long, baby-fine blonde hair was braided between his shoulder blades. Mind, he was still wearing what Heath thought of as Colin's uniform — a heavy metal tee shirt and old blue jeans — but at least the jeans had no tears or paint stains, and neither did the shirt.

Now Heath could only hope the shirt didn't have any ... questionable imagery.

Heath opened the door and was greeted by the cherry and hibiscus scents and broad smile of his grandmother.

Nana Cyr stood only maybe half a foot shorter than Heath, which made her on the north side of five-and-a-half feet tall. She was a big woman, always had been. Not fat, but solid. She was wearing her lovely purple traveling dress, which brought out highlights in her deep ebony skin. Her short waves of snowy white hair were tucked under the dress' matching pillbox hat.

On her arm was a black handbag nearly as large as Heath's backpack, and probably just as full of interesting stuff.

"There he is!" Nana Cyr said, allowing Heath to take her arm and help her out of the car.

As though the woman needed help. Heath could feel the impressive strength in her arm and legs as she stood.

He felt it even more when she wrapped him in a tight hug that threatened his ribs.

When she finally let go, Heath didn't even get to say his proper hello yet before she asked, "Now, where is this girlfriend of yours? I've been looking forward to meeting her."

"Nari's—" Heath didn't even get the second word out before the stellar jays in the nearby Japanese maple went quiet.

His grandmother turned sharply to look at them, then turned an incisive look at Heath and raised one eyebrow.

He nodded.

"Well, I'm sure I'll enjoy meeting her when I can," she said carefully.

Heath took that opportunity to introduce Tony, who looked immensely pleased that Nana Cyr asked him for a blessing after the introduction.

Colin, meanwhile, had closed the trunk, but he wasn't carrying any suitcases.

No, he was holding a well-taped cardboard box emblazoned with at least a dozen "fragile" stickers. And he was carrying it as though it weighed half of nothing, which was probably a good thing. A pale, skinny boy like Colin didn't weigh much more than half of nothing his own self.

"Shall we go inside for some coffee?" Heath asked.

"That sounds divine," Nana Cyr said, giving Heath her arm and letting him lead the way.

Heath chatted casually about the birds and plants, just to have something to talk about until it was safe to really talk, as they went. But he noticed his grandmother was at least as interested in checking out his wards and guardians as she was about the Oregon native plants in the area.

Just as interested in the small tribute to Papa Legba on Heath's white door: a black, equal-armed cross, and an old-fashioned key.

Heath opened the door and immediately wished he hadn't.

Off to the right, inside, was the big living room, which was really more of a workshop.

Oh, it had a big, wall-mounted flatscreen television — a gift from Colin — with a leather loveseat positioned before it. And, of course, Heath's big, fancy, heating and massaging leather recliner.

But that was about as much "living room" as could be seen.

And the workshop side of things, that was a *mess*.

Biggest piece of furniture in the room was the huge, solid oak workbench. Currently covered in the detritus of the morning's efforts. Spills of powder and chopped herbs. All three mortars and pestles were still either still coated in residue or paste. Chopping knives, awls, engraving tools and others clearly scattered and not organized.

Even a couple of his personal notebooks were sitting there, open, on the workbench, instead of with the rest of his personal conjure library in the walnut bookcases against the wall.

At least the herbs that hung from the ceiling to dry looked organized. So he didn't look like a *complete* slob. And none of Heath's ingredients had fallen down to the hardwood floor. Another small plus.

Still. Right now, the apartment didn't have its proper herbal smells either, because Heath had left the dregs of his coffee on.

The odor of burnt coffee. Really not what Heath needed right now.

Hell, even his breakfast dishes sat on the blonde, pressboard kitchen table where he'd left them in his hurry.

Nana Cyr didn't say a word. She just made the small sound of disapproval that Heath knew all too well.

Instantly he felt like he was fifteen again and had managed to leave the bathroom a royal mess.

"So," Tony said, "I'll get started on the coffee."

He stepped past briskly, and even managed to sweep up Heath's breakfast dishes without breaking stride.

It was a thoughtful gesture, made at the wrong time.

"Heath," Nana Cyr asked in a frosty tone, "do you usually allow your friends to do your cleaning?"

"No, ma'am," Heath said, but before he could say or do anything else, Tony started talking.

"Mrs. Cyr, I've known Heath a few months now, and I can honestly say I've never seen his apartment in such a state."

Clever words. Tony'd never been in Heath's apartment before at all.

"Me either, Mrs. Cyr," Colin said, "and I've known Heath about as long as anybody in Portland. He's usually very good at cleaning as he goes."

Nana Cyr walked over the workbench and looked at the residue of Heath's busy day. She sniffed at a couple of things, testing freshness. Glanced at the open pages of Heath's notes.

She did all of this with one eyebrow raised, but without saying a word.

In the kitchen, someone had sprayed Febreze and turned on the fan to start clearing the burnt coffee smell.

Heath started cleaning up his workbench, while she turned and looked over his bookshelves — not touching the books, just looking — then over the landscapes Heath had on the walls of his living room and kitchen. She lingered on the ones of Haiti — especially the Saut d'Eau Waterfalls — more than the ones of New Orleans.

She turned to say something else when she was interrupted by a cat.

Dr. John, Heath's two-year-old tuxedo cat, came trotting up to her, mewing like he knew there was trouble and it was his mission in life to save Heath.

Nana Cyr started laughing.

"And who might you be?" she said, scooping up the cat, who immediately started to purr like a diesel engine.

"That's Dr. John," Heath said.

"You're a smart one, aren't you?" Nana Cyr said to Dr. John as she scritched his belly. Dr. John stretched his belly as long as he could, to encourage more of this.

"Smarter than I am, most days," Heath said, stepping closer to scratch the favored spot between Dr. John's ears.

"Well, of course," Nana Cyr said. "He *is* a cat, after all. Cats rarely get caught up in business meetings or make a tenth of the mistakes we poor humans do."

"And yet," Heath said, "they put up with us."

"Coffee's brewing," Tony called from the kitchen.

"Seems to me like you have good friends," Nana Cyr whispered. "Good for you."

Nana Cyr set Dr. John down, and the cat gave Heath's legs a quick rub before trotting back toward the bedroom.

"Well," Nana Cyr said, reaching the kitchen, "that is a much more—"

She stopped, frowning. She turned toward the kitchen, where Tony had already cleaned the white oak counters and cabinets, and Colin had set the box.

But Nana Cyr's frown deepened.

She turned an angry eye on Heath, then marched right across the kitchen in the same instant that Heath realized what she'd sensed.

Mind you, Heath hadn't realized she *could* sense it. Colin and Tony sure showed no idea that they knew it was there. Heath himself, well, he hadn't quite *forgotten* it, but he *had* been trying to put off having to *deal with* it.

Nana Cyr marched right to the end cabinet, crouched down, and dug behind the set of sea green mixing bowls that had been part of the matching dishware set Nariko had bought him.

She pulled out a tin flask and held it up.

"Boy," she said in her don't-bullshit-me tone, "just *what* are you doing with a Ghede's flask?"

<hr>

"WELL," COLIN SAID, RUBBING HIS HANDS TOGETHER. "I THINK THAT'S our cue to leave. Tony?"

Tony, still standing right beside the coffee maker, which was even now starting to put out the scent of good, strong coffee, shook his head slowly.

Tony turned his gaze to Heath, but Heath kept his eyes on Nana Cyr.

She was still standing at the far end of Heath's kitchen, holding up the tin flask like she'd taken if off a student at a high school dance. That frown set in her face looked as though it might never shift again.

But Heath, he'd been through so much already today that he didn't have any trouble keeping his voice level, or his heartbeat steady.

"Please, Nana," Heath said, gesturing to the kitchen table. "Have a seat. I'll explain."

She didn't move for a moment. Then she touched two fingers to the flask and closed her eyes.

An eternal moment passed.

She opened her eyes and nodded once.

"Brav," she said, identifying the Ghede who owned that flask as though doing so was the easiest task in the world, though even Uncle Andre couldn't have done it. "All right. Could be a lot worse, but that doesn't mean you're off the hook." She strode across the hardwood floor and took the offered seat, her heels clicking along the way like the final seconds before a midnight execution — Heath's.

Heath took the other chair. That left Colin and Tony standing, but neither looked like he objected. In fact, Tony was pouring the coffee, and Colin was rooting around for cookies or something to serve with the coffee.

He found some of Heath's walnut bread and started slicing it up to serve.

"A few months back," Heath said, "the *Black Book of Saint Cyprian* tried to kill me—"

"Just *what* were you doing fooling around with an evil book like that?"

"I wasn't..." Heath steadied himself through a deep breath. "I got put into a position where I had to recover it for a client or allow Uncle Andre to get it."

Nana Cyr had a way of setting her lips that somehow conveyed an avalanche of anger just waiting to rumble down.

"Who'd you give it to then?"

Oh, that *tone,* too. Damballah knew that woman's voice could cut steel when she wanted it to. But before Heath could rally together his explanation, Tony spoke up.

"The Church," he said in a simple, but firm voice. "That was how I came to meet your grandson. He, Colin and Nariko tracked down my order — the Protective Order of Saint Benedict — and tracking us down is no easy feat, I might add. He brought the tome to us, that we might safeguard it."

"And?" she said, and Heath was grateful to hear that *tone* turned another direction for a change.

Tony held firm to his own voice though.

"The head of my order organized a special mission squad to get the book back to the Vatican's ... special vaults ... where it will remain for the foreseeable future."

Nana Cyr considered that through a long, slow breath through her nose, then nodded for Heath to continue.

"Anyway, the book failed to kill me. I found myself in the place between, talking to Brav. In order to get back, I had to burn my way through some magic."

"And Brav gave you a sip of rum to spit the fire." Nana Cyr nodded. "That's good. Good of him to do it, and good of you to handle it. And good of you to get that book back in the Church's hands."

She turned an accusing eye on Tony. "Even if they *were* the ones who let it escape in the first place."

"A mistake that will not be repeated," Tony said with a slight bow, "I assure you."

"When I came back," Heath continued, trying to get through this story in one piece, "I was still holding the flask. Did Uncle Andre—"

"Tell me you bested him?" Nana Cyr flashed a quick smile. "Oh, he tried to spin it, but I figured out you tricked him. Involved the flask, did it?"

"Yes, ma'am."

"Explains why Brav let you hold onto it. But why do you still have it?"

"Well, for one, I haven't been sure how to get it back to him."

"And for two?"

Heath drew a breath and let it out. "I figured he let me hold onto it because he had something in mind for when I returned it. Rental fee of some kind, as it were." Heath hung his head. "I've been a little worried about what that might be."

Nana Cyr shook her head. "Boy, you will *never* be a *houngan* if you're afraid of the Lwa."

"I'll never be a *houngan* because I'm not..."

Heath let those words drift off at the sight of his grandmother's raised eyebrows.

"Am I?"

"I was so furious at Andre for what he'd done," Nana Cyr said, speaking for the first time about when Heath's uncle had tried to offer him up in sacrifice to Baron Samedi. "Had he not been my own flesh and blood..."

Nana Cyr's nostrils flared wide in an angry breath, but her words were calmer afterwards.

"Remember how sick you were when you came back from his farm?"

"Do I," Heath said with a sigh. "His little stunt with that makeshift grave gave me pneumonia. I remember you gave me…"

"Go on," Nana Cyr said.

"All those baths," Heath said with growing realization. "And you kept praying and singing over me with those herbs and concoctions. And—"

"That's all you need to say aloud," Nana Cyr said firmly. "You get my point, and there are those present, well meaning as they may be, who don't have the right to hear about this in any more detail than that."

"You mean—"

"I *mean*," Nana Cyr said, "that you did not have pneumonia in the least. That fever you had, that was Papa Legba marking you as one of his own, and making sure I knew to make you *hounsi kanzo* straight away."

Hounsi kanzo. The full initiation ceremony of Vodou. Only the first initiation, true, but more of an initiation than most *vodouisants* would need in their lifetimes. People only went through the time, expense, and trouble to become *kanzo*…

…under extraordinary circumstances.

Just then, Heath was sure he could hear three things that weren't any kind of physical noise at all.

The first was the cane of Papa Legba, tapping in approval. The second, the laughter of Ghede Brav. The third, Brav's smoky skulls chanting "ding ding ding ding ding."

"Normally I never would have done it," Nana Cyr said, still talking even though Heath suspected, from the tilt of her head, that she heard those … other sounds too. "Not with you being so young as you were. But you'd already made your own deal with Legba, and he insisted on the *kanzo* as part of it."

She frowned and shook her head. "He was right, too. I may not have been sure of it at the time, but seeing the way you and Andre have been since then, how could I really doubt it?"

"I never wanted conflict with my uncle."

"No," Nana Cyr said with a sigh. "I know that. And if we're all lucky, you won't have any again. He respects you now. But with Andre, respect might be as hazardous for you as dismissal."

Tony took that moment to set down cups of coffee, as well as cream, sugar, and other sweeteners.

Impressive, how quickly Tony had made himself at home.

Heath added both cream and sugar to the coffee. He needed them, right now. Nana Cyr did the same, but settled for fake sugar.

Colin laid out the walnut bread, and Nana Cyr's face lit up.

"Is this my recipe?"

Heath smiled and nodded.

She bit into a slice and looked positively transported by the rich, moist taste. "Boy, your baking has *improved*. That is just the *perfect* touch of molasses. And that kiss of cinnamon. Mmm."

Heath was just about to pounce on that subject change when his grandmother raised an eyebrow and continued, "But we need to talk about this flask."

"I know," Heath said, "I need to get it back to him. But before I can do that, I need to figure out what it means that I'm *kanzo*. I need to—"

"You need to accept that you're the same man you were this morning when you got dressed." Nana Cyr shook her head. "The Lwa knew all along, even if I might have … elided over a few of the details."

Did Heath's grandmother actually look a little embarrassed?

Hard to say. He'd never seen her embarrassed before.

"If I may interject," Tony said softly, "this might be a secondary matter in light of what happened a few minutes ago."

Heath's turn to give someone a furious look. But Tony, he just weathered it like Heath's anger wasn't a thing to concern him.

Or maybe as though he knew that, however angry Heath got, he was unlikely to just strike out at Tony without better cause than *that*.

Nana Cyr turned an expectant eye on Heath.

Colin was standing behind Heath, leaning against the counter opposite Tony. So Heath couldn't see Colin even a little. But he could *feel* the curiosity burning out of Colin.

Heath told about the assassination attempt simple and straight, and didn't hide any of it.

When he finished, Nana Cyr sipped her coffee for a moment. Took another bite of bread.

"Well," she said at last, "I don't agree with Andre about much. But I will say he's right about one thing. You *are* a proper conjure man, if a gunman you don't know is coming can't get a clear shot at you on a city sidewalk in broad daylight with surprise on his side."

"Pretty sure that conjure hand is *done*," Heath said. "Wasn't built to turn away that many gunshots."

Nana Cyr nodded as though Heath hadn't said anything surprising.

"Well," she said at last. "Guess it's a good thing I'm here. Let's talk about how we get you out of this mess."

Funny, what a difference just talking can make.

When Heath got home from that little business meeting, he'd been shaken. Borderline in shock. And yet, just the chance to sit in his kitchen for a little bit, eating walnut bread and drinking coffee and talking with his grandmother...

All right, Colin and Tony were here, but they'd been smart enough to leave most of the conversation so far to Heath and Nana.

Anyway, this had done just the trick Heath needed. Given him a little space. A little perspective. A chance to let some pieces jiggle together in his head until they fit a picture that made one hell of a lot more sense than he'd thought it did even just half an hour ago.

Oh, he didn't suddenly have all the answers or anything. Heath knew himself and his life well enough to know both those things.

Hell, he knew that even what he *suspected* might be wrong. But that didn't matter. Not really.

Because Heath, he had a starting point now. He'd remembered some very important details from events of the past year.

So Heath, he did what he always liked to do when he had one of those moments where everything seemed to come together.

He took a few seconds to just enjoy it. Didn't come around often enough, so moments like these were to be *savored*.

So Heath enjoyed the sense of calm that came over him then. The settling in his belly and the certainty in his mind, after the chaos his day had been so far.

All told, a good feeling. A feeling that allowed Heath to enjoy the taste of his walnut bread even more. The hint of molasses, the tiniest dash of cinnamon, both only highlights in the moist, delicious taste.

A taste that was brought out even more by his coffee. A good, Puerto Rican blend, liberally dosed right now with cream and sugar.

Such a good moment that, well, Heath hated to say what he knew he had to say right then to his grandmother's blatant offer of help.

But Heath needed to get the ball rolling again, and that was how it had to start.

"No, ma'am."

Nana Cyr gave Heath the long, slow blink. It was a look he'd seen many times in his life. It was her giving Heath a chance to reconsider his words, and determine whether or not he *really* wanted to say what he'd just said.

"Nana," Heath said, setting down his coffee cup and taking her free hand in his, "you came to visit, and I am truly glad you're here. I love you, and it's wonderful to see you. I can't wait to introduce you to Nariko, and show you around town. To sit and talk with you about your life and mine."

Heath shook his head, a little self-deprecating. "And if, while you're here, you have time to help me get that flask back to Ghede Brav without digging myself a pit in the process, well, I would truly appreciate that. I'd be a damned fool to turn down the aid of a strong, experienced *manbo* such as yourself in dealing with the Lwa."

He shook his head again, but this time slow and firm. "But this gunman, he's *my* problem. And now that I've had a moment to think, I realize he's not even a *new* problem. Just an old problem I wasn't expecting to pop up. Not now, and certainly not the way it has."

He leaned in a little closer. "Now I could be wrong about this, though I don't think I am. Either way, though, I am *not* going to put you in harm's way trying to help me."

"You're saying you don't want my help?"

That ... that was a tone Heath didn't recognize. Didn't sound angry or sad or accusatory or even curious. And worse, Heath couldn't read anything more in the woman's posture or expression.

She'd made those words very, very careful. Which meant they might be a test of some kind. But if so, Heath didn't know what kind of test, or what it meant.

So all he could do was answer honestly.

"I'm saying I don't want your help enough to put you at risk. But let me say a little bit more about all this."

A single nod. A simple down-up motion to her chin that could have meant anything or nothing at all, and Heath wasn't sure which.

He inhaled slowly through his nose, and didn't think about that breath again as he spoke.

"I've had someone come after me with gunfire today, and I have to admit, it threw me more than I wanted it to."

"Heath," Tony started in a don't-blame-yourself kind of tone, but let his words trail off at a gesture from Heath.

"But now that I'm not *actively ducking* a shooter," Heath continued, "I've realized that while this was, indeed, the first time I've been *shot* at, it's not in fact the first time I've had a gun pointed at me. Not even the first time that's happened this year."

"Quite a year you're having," Nana Cyr said, one eyebrow high.

"You're telling me," Heath said.

"The trench coat brigade," Colin said suddenly, the force of realization carrying him forward a step.

"The trench coat brigade," Heath confirmed.

"What's the trench coat brigade?" Tony asked.

"Don't they work for your landlord?" Colin asked.

"Your *landlord*?" Nana said, fury in her tone. "Your *landlord* is trying to kill you?"

"Hold up," Heath said, raising his hands for peace.

His grandmother shifted angrily in her seat through a long, fast breath, but nodded for Heath to speak.

"Now it *could* be my landlord, but I don't think so." At the impatient look on his grandmother's face, Heath took a moment to explain. "He's the one who hired me on the Saint Cyprian thing. Rich boy with underworld connections who wanted to add magic to his résumé."

Heath shook his head. "By the time that little affair was over, I'm pretty sure he understood that if he ever came after me and got lucky, he could expect the rest of his life to be short, and very unpleasant. Not to mention an afterlife that I think he'd just as soon avoid."

"Oh?" Tony asked, tone a little too casual.

"Wasn't just Nariko and Colin making the point. Uncle Andre kind of ... underscored it."

"Andre does love his zombies," Nana Cyr said sadly.

Heath turned to Tony, who was frowning. Considering.

"As for who the trench coat brigade is, they're about what they sound like. Guys in trench coats, with firearms. All of 'em looking and acting like organized crime types."

"And they showed up at my house, supporting your landlord," Colin said. "Half dozen of them. Clearly in his employ."

"That's part of what threw me," Heath admitted, shaking an index finger. "But they weren't the first guys in trench coats we had to deal with. And the earlier ones, they were trying to stop me from getting the book, which meant they couldn't have been working for my landlord."

"The big brawl at the Witch's Castle," Colin said, referring to the old building in Forest Park that had become one of the points of power around Portland. "Had a bunch of those trench coat guys."

"Yep," Heath said. "And Suit wouldn't have sent them. Would have been counterproductive, considering the number of other players coming after the book."

"Suit?" Tony asked, then nodded as though he should have guessed. "Ah. Your working nickname for your landlord."

"Exactly," Heath said.

"So whoever sent the trench coat brigade after us at the Witch's Castle," Colin said. "*That's* who tried to kill you?" He shook his head. "Not a lot to go on."

"No," Heath said, smiling now, "but that wasn't the first time a guy in a trench coat came looking for me. In fact, that one was carrying a submachine gun."

Colin slapped himself in the forehead. "Of course."

"He had a *look-at-me* charm on that trench coat," Heath said, "same as his two partners, who tried to distract me while a snapper tried to kill me. Just proving they had magical ties. More evidence suggesting they weren't working for Suit."

"Snapper?" Tony asked.

"Angry spirit," Nana Cyr said offhandedly, "bound into the shape of a bird. Pretty deadly."

"This was all months ago," Colin said. "No way a spell's going to be able to trace those guys now."

Heath chuckled and shook his head, while his grandmother smiled and met his eyes, sharing his amusement.

She let Heath explain.

"Legwork is usually a better starting point than magic," Heath said. "And in this case, we know someone who probably got a lot of good information out of one of these guys. After all, she clearly wanted to teach him a lesson."

"Inga," Colin said, smiling now. He rubbed his hands together. "Good. I haven't had a *pirozhki* in weeks."

"How do you stay so skinny?" Nana Cyr said, looking Colin up and down as he picked up his fifth slice of walnut bread. "You never stop eating."

"Trade secret," Colin said, waggling his eyebrows.

"Well," Nana Cyr said with an air of finality. "If you're not going to let me come along and help, at least let me clean up this mess. Maybe take advantage of your pantry, with your kind permission."

"Ooh," Colin said, "Heath's bragged about your beignets."

"That's not the pantry she's talking about," Heath said, nodding over toward his workbench. "But, Nana, my house is your house. Conjure if you like. Bake if you like. Whatever you want to do. In fact…"

Heath cleared his throat a special way, which would draw the attention of all the spirits and guardians he had inside his wards.

"Now hear this," Heath said in a loud, clear voice. "This woman is my own grandmother, blood of my blood. Take a sniff, so you know her."

Nana Cyr sat straight and patient while a series of spirits drifted past, developing a sense of who and what she was, tasting a little drop of her magic, so they could recognize her again.

"Anything she wants to do," Heath continued, "is fine with me. Help her if she asks, stay out of her way if she prefers, but do not impede her."

Heath had functionally just given his grandmother the skeleton key to most of his magic, and she knew it. Tears actually touched the edges of Nana Cyr's eyes then, she was so moved.

"You don't have to—"

"There's no one I trust more," Heath said. "So you make yourself at home."

He turned to Colin and Tony.

"Now we should get going."

"Not until you see what I have for you," she said, pointing to the box Colin had carried in. "Might be something in there you could use."

UNBELIEVABLE, JUST HOW DISTRACTING IT HAD BEEN TO HAVE HEATH'S grandmother sitting in his own kitchen. He'd forgotten all about that box she'd had Colin carry in, even though it was sitting on the counter not ten feet away.

Practically in his line of sight. If he happened to look over at

Colin, anyway. He stood in front of it, but a skinny guy like Colin couldn't hide much with just his body.

The box was about as wide as Heath's forearm was long, and just about that same distance in height. In length, just a skosh longer. Maybe his elbow to his fingertips.

Taped solidly closed with packing tape, with at least three packages' shares of "fragile" stickers scattered around it.

What was more, Heath could feel that there was a charm or two involved in closing it up and handling its shipping. Making sure that nothing inside it got hurt even a little bit.

He cocked an eyebrow at Nana, making sure he was all right to open it. She smiled indulgently and nodded.

Heath pulled a folding knife from a pants pocket. Not his best knife, by any stretch. Hell, not even the best knife he carried, when he had his backpack with him.

But this one had a bunch of little tools on it that came in handy more times than Heath bothered keeping track of. And as far as cutting open a box went, it would do the job just fine.

And it did. Sliced right through the tape like it was a scalpel, moonlighting on its night off.

Inside the flaps, packing peanuts.

Colin started laughing at the sight of all that polystyrene.

"Bet you could get arrested for having those. This is Portland, after all."

"You *must* be joking," Nana Cyr said.

"Hey," Heath said, without looking away from the box. "Not like they're straws or utensils. Perfectly legal, last I heard."

"If the box were shipped commercially," Tony added, "might be a different matter. This though. Should be fine."

"Just what kind of town is this, Heath?" Nana Cyr asked.

Heath smiled at her.

"Notice all those trees you passed between the airport and here?"

She raised her eyebrows to indicate that it was a foolish question.

"Not positive," Heath said, "but I think they all have the vote. Wouldn't surprise me if some of them held office."

Nana snorted a laugh, but it was a laugh Heath knew. A laugh that said he was crazy, but she understood the truth behind what he was saying.

Colin held up his hands as though to say he'd made his point.

Heath shook his head, chuckling a little himself, and began to dig inside the box.

He was spilling those stupid packing peanuts, but as long as Dr. John didn't try to run off with them, that was fine.

Just how deep did he have to dig though?

There. Finally.

Suspended in a tight coil of bubble wrap and rubber bands near the bottom of the box, a smaller box.

Heath cocked an eyebrow at his grandmother as he extracted that smaller box, but her face showed nothing but simmering pleasure.

Whatever was in this box, she was enjoying giving it to him.

The inner box weighed almost as much as the whole package. Only maybe eight inches long, four across, and two deep.

The urge to shake it was maddening, but Heath knew better.

There are lots of gifts in this world that can be shaken. Some are even *meant* to be shaken. But a gift from a conjure woman — a *manbo* no less — that was not one of them.

Colin already had Heath's dustpan and broom, ready to sweep up the peanuts, so Heath brought the smaller box to the table and let Colin handle that quick.

He waited until Colin was finished and watching again, before proceeding.

Heath slit the tape open, then uncoiled the bubble wrap while keeping the little box level and upright.

Now that he could see it better, during the unwrapping, the box was made of thin wood.

An old fashioned cigar box. Brand was El Rey Del Mundo, and a faint odor of cigars remained, though Heath had no doubt that there hadn't been any cigars in his box in decades.

There was power inside the box. He could feel it. *Pwen*, they would have called it back in Louisiana.

He set the box on the table. Reached to slide the top open—

—and stopped himself.

He frowned. Looked up at his grandmother.

"There's something has to be done, before this box can be opened safely. Isn't there."

He didn't even try to make it sound like a question.

Nana Cyr's smile widened. She turned to Colin and Tony. "Why don't you two boys wait outside for a few? I'll send Heath out when he's ready."

Colin's face fell like Nana Cyr just canceled Christmas. Tony, though, he nodded as though he'd been expecting the request. He took Colin by the arm, handed him a consolation slice of walnut bread, and guided him toward the front door.

Colin turned back just as Tony opened the door.

"You'll tell us what's in it though, Heath. Right?"

Heath gave an apologetic shrug. "Depends on what's in it."

Colin sighed and hung his head, while Tony helped him outside.

Once the door was closed, Heath asked, "You going to tell me how to open it? Or do I have to guess?"

"You already know," she said. "You just don't know you know."

Heath blinked the question.

"We were talking a little bit ago about your *kanzo*. Do you remember, during those baths and songs, when I gave you a secret word? A word just for us?"

Heath nodded.

"That's kind of like a special password. Not the one I used to use when I had a congregation, but a special one picked out for you by Papa Legba. You say it or think it as you open the box, and you can do it safely every time. And that goes for any other special things I might give you in the coming years."

"Special things?"

"Don't you worry about that now. You open your box."

Heath thought that password nice and clear as he slid open the lid.

Three things inside that box. Besides that faint odor of cigars.

The first was a rosary made from alternating beads, different shades of white, with a silver crucifix. The second was a plastic bag containing seven ... snake vertebrae if Heath guessed right.

The third was a finger. Well, the bones of one, anyway, all the way up to the third joint (which was not included).

Power just sort of oozed out of all three. Very different power from each.

"The snake bones," Nana Cyr said in a crisp, businesslike tone, leaning forward now and pointing, "are for your *asson*, when you finally become a *houngan*."

The *asson*, a rattle made from a type of gourd, was a major tool in the hands of any *manbo* or *houngan*.

"I haven't agreed to—"

"The rosary," she continued, "has been handed down since my grandmother's grandfather's grandfather." She cocked an eyebrow. "And I do hope you'll have some grandchildren of your own to pass it down to one day."

"Conversation for another time?" Heath said, hopefully.

Nana Cyr made a small sound of disapproval, but continued.

"This rosary was a gift from Damballah, and has been thrice blessed by Him."

Damballah. If any of the Lwa could be called "the holiest" it would be Damballah.

"And the finger bone?"

"That, my dear, is a true religious artifact. That is none other than the finger bone of Saint Homobonus."

Homobonus. Homobonus. Heath tried to remember, but he found that difficult while staring at an actual human finger bone. Finger bones. Whatever the proper term was.

Closing his eyes was enough, though, to clear the distraction and bring the answer quickly to mind.

Knowing all the saints and their domains was important to his conjure work. And since most saints had more than one, quickly identifying the *right* domain was just as important.

"The patron saint of businesspeople?"

"That's him," she said. "And I have confirmed its authenticity myself. Just *having* it is going to give your business a boost. As for what else you can do with it..." Nana Cyr smiled. "I'm sure you'll think of a few things."

"Do I want to know how you came by this?"

"Gift from a *very* happy client."

For a moment — just one fleeting *moment* — Heath was tempted to ask for details. His grandmother might even have given them.

But any client happy enough to *give* the finger bone of a *saint* as a gift — not a payment, a gift on top of payment — that client must have needed some major juju.

Heath wasn't sure that was a story he wanted to hear.

"This..." he said, returning to more important points just then, "this is too much, Nana. Don't you need these things yourself?"

"I don't take clients anymore," she said, pointing to the finger bone. While pointing at the other two, she continued, "the snake bones it was past time to give you, and the rosary, well, I do hope it will help you live long enough to have grandchildren you can pass it down to yourself one day..."

"Thank you, Nana. Thank you more than I can even guess at how to say. Any one of these gifts would be amazing. But all three?"

Heath shook his head. "I just feel too blessed for words."

"Not too blessed for hugs, I hope."

"Not at all," Heath said, slipping the rosary into a pocket. He closed the cigar box, then, and gave his grandmother a hug that tried to tell her just how grateful he was.

It fell short, in Heath's opinion, but he hoped she got the message anyway.

After the hug, he tucked the cigar box into a cabinet nobody but he — and now his grandmother — would ever think to look inside, thanks to some of Heath's more subtle work.

As he scooped up his backpack and said his goodbye, his grandmother commented, "Might not want to mention that finger bone to your monk friend."

"Wouldn't dream of it," he said with a wink.

HEATH DIDN'T GET TWO STEPS INTO THE AFTERNOON HEAT BEFORE Colin was in his face. His words a cloud of walnut and molasses from all the bread.

"Dish! I gotta know! *What was in the box?*"

"I tried, Heath," Tony said, standing up from one of the two chairs Heath kept on his porch. "I must have tried fifteen different topics, but..."

He gestured helplessly.

Colin just looked so frustrated and eager and desperate. Like Dr. John, when his favorite catnip mouse got stuck under the couch, and he could only wail and wail for Heath to come fix the problem.

The comparison got Heath laughing, which was not the reaction Colin was looking for.

"Spill it. Spill it. Spill it. Spill it."

"All right, all right, I give," Heath said, still laughing as he dipped his hand into his pocket. "You can look, but you can't touch. This little baby is still getting to know me, and I don't want anyone touching it until I've had it at least ... oh ... let's say a month."

Colin nodded rapidly and backed off a step, his hands behind his back now.

Heath pulled out the rosary. Held it up by one finger, so it dangled and the silver caught the sun.

"Wow," Colin said, blinking. "Lotta juice in that little baby."

"Interesting color choices," Tony said, leaning forward a little and also keeping his hands behind his back. "Damballah?"

"Yes," Heath said, a little suspiciously. He knew Tony's order kept up with lots of religions that had magical aspects, but he didn't expect that level of detail.

"Just a guess," Tony said. "I remembered the two rosaries you'd wrapped the *Black Book of Saint Cyprian* in, both blessed in the name of Damballah."

"Well," Heath said, "this one's been in the family a lot longer."

"And there was more than one thing in that box," Colin said. "Three things, if my senses weren't lying."

"They weren't," Heath said, sighing with both exasperation and a bit of pleasure that his friend was sharp enough to have picked out three distinct auras of power before the box was even open.

"Second was a baggie of potent snake bones."

"What are those for?" Colin asked.

"Your *asson* one day?" Tony said, both answering Colin and asking Heath.

Heath gave Tony a frank look that got a smile out of the monk.

"Hey, I do know a thing or two about Vodou."

"What's the third?"

"The third," Heath said with a smile, "is just a little something to help with my business."

"A *gris-gris*?" Colin asked, remembering to use the right term for the kind of charms Heath made.

"Something like that," Heath said, slipping the rosary back into his pocket, "but that's enough show and tell for now. Let's go."

3

The restaurant called Tsarina's was tucked away in the industrial part of northwest Portland, close to the Willamette River.

If you didn't know Tsarina's was there, you'd drive past it without suspecting. If you *did* know, you might still need a couple of laps to spot it.

Didn't look like a restaurant, from the outside. Looked like every other office building around it. Like one of those miniature airplane hangars. That kind of aluminum construction and rounded, sloped roof. Maybe as long as a railcar.

All the neighborhood buildings in that style came in the kinds of colors usually found in ice cream shops. Tsarina's was … mint. Maybe pistachio.

The lot it sat on had the same kind of cyclone fence topped with razor wire as all the other lots around it. Lots full of semis and buses. Lots with alarms, and sometimes guard dogs.

Heath used to think that Tsarina's leased their space from a lot that didn't need its little office building.

Lately, though. Lately he'd started thinking maybe it was a front for the Russian mob.

Inside, Tsarina's did look like a restaurant, but one done on the cheap. Narrow as the building was, it only had one row of tables, all butted up against one of its long walls.

Folding tables, with folding chairs. Tablecloths checked with red and white. The only nod to decoration — each table had a vase. Right now those vases held purple Gerber daisies.

The wall beside the "walkway" that led to the counter and the back was decorated with old photos of a Russian royal family that no longer existed, far as Heath knew.

Actual photos, too. Not cutouts from magazines or newspapers. Not even printouts on modern printer paper.

Actual photos. As though somebody involved with Tsarina's actually had *that* kind of connection.

As opposed to the other kind. Which was only cemented in Heath's mind as he squeaked open the aluminum screen door and saw what he always saw when he entered Tsarina's.

Two tables at the back, full of old men talking in Russian.

Only nine chairs available for customers who weren't old Russian men. And, much like most of the other times Heath had come in, all three of those tables were empty...

Well, Tsarina's might have been a front, but it was definitely a restaurant. The big portable fan in the kitchen was wafting out more heat, accompanying the delightful smells of Russian cooking.

Heath took his usual seat — first table in, the seat watching the front door. Colin sat facing him. Tony hovered for a moment.

"Bathroom in the back?" he asked.

Heath and Colin looked at each other. Heath answered.

"Wait and ask Inga."

Tony frowned, but sat. Moments later, loud Russian conversation from the kitchen.

Heath heard the steady complaint of the aluminum floor, and knew Inga was approaching at her usual marching pace.

Inga was what Heath's grandmother would call a big woman. And maybe it was the Russian theme of the place, but Heath always thought she looked kind of like a potato, right down to the blotchy skin.

No brown dress today, though, which helped shift the image. A dark red look today, so more like a beet, if someone piled long braids of yellow-blond hair on its top.

"Is late lunch or early dinner?" Inga asked.

"Not quite ready to order yet," Tony said. "Could I use your restroom?"

Inga frowned at him. Looked him up and down. Tsarina's didn't let just any customer use their restroom. If they didn't like you, it was always mysteriously out of order.

"Heath, Colin," she said, "who is this? Friend of yours?"

"This is Father Antonio," Heath said. "A good friend of ours."

"You vouch for him then?"

"To use the bathroom?" Tony asked, voice full of disbelief.

"Definitely," Heath said, in the same moment Colin said, "Absolutely."

Inga nodded. "Is in the back. Second door. Not first. *Not* third. Second."

"Right," Tony said, still a bit bemused about the mysteries of Tsarina's restroom, but he made his way down the loud, aluminum floor quickly.

"Does he take his coffee American-weak like you?" Inga asked Heath in a tone far more free of judgment than her words. "Or Russian-strong like your Nariko?"

Heath sighed, hoping Nariko was all right. Only a couple of hours before dark now, and he still hadn't heard from her. He yearned to call her, but knew it was a bad idea. She'd call when she could.

"Tony's a Catholic monk," Colin said. "Assume he takes his coffee as strong as his beer."

Inga nodded, apparently finding more information in that answer than Heath did.

"So," she said. "Still waiting. Is late lunch or early dinner?"

"Late lunch," Colin said, before Heath could say otherwise.

"So lunch *pirozhki* for Heath" — which meant beef, cabbage, potatoes and a little cheese — "and your usual, Colin?"

Colin grinned. His lunchtime usual was enough to feed a family of four.

"What about your friend the priest?"

Heath was pretty sure he heard a frown in her voice.

"Tony," Heath said, hoping a proper name would ... ease whatever opinion Inga held of Catholic priests. "Lunch *pirozhki*. If he doesn't want it, I'll take it to go."

Inga nodded and made her way back. The walkway was narrow enough that Tony had to let her reach the kitchen before he could return to claim his seat.

"It's just a bathroom," he said, still wondering. "Cleaner than some. Smelled like boiled beets and cabbage. What's the big deal?"

"Yeah," Colin said. "I think they're more interested in keeping questionable customers where they can watch them."

"Not a good way to keep customers coming back."

"If they don't like you," Heath said with a shrug, "they don't want you to come back."

They brought him up to speed on the order, and settled in for their meal.

Heath's idea, that. Not to ask Inga any questions until after they'd eaten and paid. He figured there was less chance of accidental offense that way.

It was when Inga returned with their change, Heath posed the question.

"Inga, remember a few months back? The guy in the trench coat with the submachine gun?"

Inga snorted. "Of course I remember. Stupid man. To come into *Tsarina's* waving a Thompson."

She shook her head. Reached out and patted Heath's shoulder with a surprisingly gentle hand.

"Have no fear in this place, Heath. We like you. You are safe here. And that man, he has learned his lesson. He will not come back."

"Someone took shots at me today. With a rifle. Sniper style."

The old men stopped talking.

Inga loomed.

She shouldn't have been able to loom properly. Sure, she had some mass, but she was a good half-foot shorter than Heath.

Nevertheless, in that moment, she got quiet and she seemed to radiate a kind of menace that was a power of its own.

Inga got scary like that sometimes.

But when she spoke, her words were careful. Not threatening.

"That business over on 20th? That was you?"

"Someone shooting *at* me, yes. With a sniper rifle, I think."

One of the old men said something in Russian. Inga nodded.

"And you don't know," she said, "*why* someone would take shots at you with a SIG Scharfschutzengewehr 3000?"

"Take shots and *miss*," one of the old men said, though Heath didn't catch which one.

"How do you know what kind of rifle?" Tony asked.

"Heath," Inga said, "tell your friend not to ask stupid questions if he wishes to dine here again."

"Tony," Heath said in a warning tone.

Tony nodded. Wary. Mimed locking his lips.

"I don't live the kind of life that gets me shot at, generally speaking," Heath said to Inga. "And since the last time it happened started the day with that incident here, I figured—"

"You figured the same people might be … involved," Inga said.

More Russian from close to the counter.

"Is fair question," Inga said with a frown. "The missing. Shots were message? Or did shooter miss because you are *vedmak*?"

"*Vedmak*?" Colin asked.

"Like a warlock or witch," Tony said softly, getting a nod of approval from Inga, followed by a suspicious look, then another, less approving nod.

"I'm pretty sure he'd've killed me if he could've," Heath said.

Inga nodded. Pulled out her steno pad just to slap it against one palm. Nodded again.

"You are good customer, Heath. And good man, I think. If you wish, we will see to this."

Heath flashed on the image of starting a gang war between the Russian mob in Portland and ... whoever was coming after him.

Not to mention that he would *owe* Inga after this.

He fought down a shudder.

"Thank you very much for the offer," Heath said, "but this is the kind of thing I should take care of myself."

"You are certain? Is never a bad thing, for your enemies to know you have friends."

"True," Heath said, "but it's even better if my enemies fear me for me, not *just* my friends."

Inga smiled that scary smile of hers. Like a wolf that just spotted prey large enough to feed the pack.

"Is good answer. You just wish information then?"

"Please."

"Of course. And maybe before you leave, you bless this place. Nothing big. Just that ... bored police find better things to look at."

Tony cleared his throat.

"This one must wait *outside*," Inga said, then turned to Tony. "Better you eat elsewhere, in the future."

"I was just thinking the same thing," Tony said, standing. "Heath, Colin, I'll see you guys by the car."

Heath waited until the front door swung shut.

"Of course," Heath said, more than happy to balance the scales on the same visit. "I'll use a variation of the little charm I use on my own car."

Inga laughed approvingly, and then she started to talk.

Brooklyn.

Back when Heath lived in Manhattan, he hadn't liked going to Brooklyn. Sure, he could have claimed that was because of the long train ride, or a difference in attitude. Really, he could have pointed to any of a dozen other things a Manhattanite might use as an excuse to look down on New York's other boroughs.

Truth was, bad experiences had soured Heath on Brooklyn. He'd been beaten up there on one trip. Mugged on another. Dumped on a third.

Dumb luck? Maybe. The first two happened before Heath started on the conjure path, so he couldn't really be sure.

But Heath's dad always said: once is bad luck, twice is coincidence, and three times is enemy action.

Whether that was true or not, Heath just sort of figured that Brooklyn wasn't a healthy place for him to go, and avoided it whenever he could.

Of course, once Heath moved to Portland, he figured he'd never have to worry about Brooklyn again.

Wrong.

Turned out, "Brooklyn" happened to be the name given to one of the neighborhoods on Portland's east side, near the river. And this Brooklyn had something to do with trying to kill him.

Heath sat there now, maybe a half-hour before dusk. In the front passenger seat of Tony's Forester. Tony behind the wheel. Colin in the back seat.

The scent of frankincense that always seemed to pervade the car didn't do anything to cut the current tension in it.

Colin wasn't fidgeting, but it was a near thing. Practically vibrated in the backseat. Wanting to say something, but not wanting to be the first to talk.

Heath could feel Tony's ambivalence. Tony's desire to "say something" to Heath about that incident in Tsarina's, warring with the fact that it had produced actionable information.

Inga had identified the group behind the trench coat brigade as Flex. As in, when you need some extra muscle, these guys will help you flex.

Flex, according to Inga's sources, was based out of a little office building on SE Milwaukie that was supposedly empty. Little gray building. Two story. Concrete stairs on both ends. Glass fronts and doors, but all the blinds drawn.

Lettering on the windows and doors for a dentist, a massage

parlor, an accountant and a physical therapist had been scraped away, but were probably still legible. If Heath got close enough.

Parking lot had eight spaces, two of them filled by mid-size sedans. Nothing too recent. Nothing too nice. Even the paint jobs looked nice and weathered.

Sign at the edge of the parking lot for Third Sun Realty claimed space was available and gave a number that Heath had already written down.

He had no doubt that anyone calling that number would be frustrated at the ridiculously high rate the landlord wanted to charge for that space, and never call again.

Assuming any interested parties called at all. Because these Flex people, they'd done a few nice tricks to the place.

First, on the lot itself.

They didn't use an *ignore-me* charm or any kind of variant. Nothing to make the eyes just slide right off the building and onto the next.

No, whoever was handling the juju for these guys took a different approach. They made the whole lot feel ... run down.

If Heath had been just an average joe looking for office space, he'd have seen the sign, maybe perked up a little at the location. But then his eyes would have settled on the building, and he would have turned away thinking it was the kind of building with faulty wiring and plumbing. Maybe stains and bad smells in the walls and carpets that would never come out. Possibly even walls that were half-spackle or something.

A building on its last legs. Not quite ready to fall over, but definitely not a place to sink money into.

Best part? All of it was just a feeling, and looking away helped that feeling slide away. Made sure the viewer felt a little better after looking away. A little happier. Maybe a little "there but for the grace of God go I."

And then, just forget about it and think about something more important. A little *extra* to make sure no one would dwell on having a rundown place in the neighborhood. Kept the neighbors from complaining about the "eyesore."

Tricky work, too. Even when Heath had opened his spirit eyes for a closer look, to see what kind of spells they'd laid in detail, they'd almost slipped another something past him.

The spells were pretty fresh, but they looked old. Like somebody'd been paid to set them up ten or twenty years ago, and so the place might really have been abandoned by now. As though the spells were just a little touch of irony these days. Maybe even kept the owners themselves from paying the property any mind.

Took patience and discernment to get past the obfuscation to the truth. But Heath, he had plenty of both.

The way Flex kept strangers from using their supposedly abandoned parking lot was even cleverer. No extra magic to it, apart from that run down feeling.

The Flex people just conspicuously left broken safety glass in several of the parking spaces. As though parking there was likely to lead to broken windows and robbed cars.

Might have been a couple of rusty razor blades and broken syringes too. Couldn't tell that much from down the street, where Tony'd parked.

Add little details like those to the feel of the lot and building overall, and Heath had no doubt that the two sedans parked there belonged to Flex.

Very little magic to the cars. Just a *touch* on the license plates. Made them a little harder to focus on. Blurred their letters just enough to get them wrong, but only if someone was actually trying to mark them.

Subtle work, that. With so much else going on, Heath might not have noticed if he hadn't wanted to write down the plate numbers when they'd driven past.

"Gotta say," Heath said. "Does seem like the kind of place that would send out guys with *look-at-me* charms to distract me from an incoming snapper."

"Heath," Tony said, probably glad not to have to speak first. "I know you live in a gray area in many respects—"

Heath's phone broke into the opening notes of "Dans Kalinda Ba Boom" by Dr. John.

"That's Nariko," he said, and Tony was smart enough to shut up while Heath answered. "Nari. Everything okay?"

"I should be asking you. Someone's shooting at you?"

Heath frowned, then realized he heard his grandmother's voice in the background. Nariko must have gone straight to his place, and of course Nana Cyr let her in...

"Hired guns. We're staking out their place of business right now."

"Without me?"

She sounded so plaintive that apologies fell out of Heath's mouth before he could even mention that she'd been out of town. Or that she had plenty on her plate, trying to figure out how to deal with her mother — a freaking *earth dragon* of all things. Or any of a number of other points he could have raised.

But the first apology was barely past his lips before she spoke over him.

"Never mind that right now. I'm at your place, and we need to bring each other up to speed. In person."

"On our way."

Heath nodded at Tony. Tony fired up his Subaru, reminding Heath just a little that for all the *real* drama his life had, he was woefully short of *cinematic* drama.

A friend he was arguing with was firing up a car to take them from the business place of hit men for hire, back to his home to hear how the daughter of an immortal dragon was going to escape her mother.

He should have been riding in a car that *vroomed* to life, kicking off a soundtrack that would move audiences to the edge of their seats. Maybe peeling out, just as gunshots fired off, or something exploded in the background.

Heath shook his head as the Subaru purred to wakefulness and glided away from the curb into gentle, late afternoon traffic.

What the hell had he just been thinking? Wanting *more* drama in his life?

Clearly Heath needed more sleep.

AT LEAST THE DRIVE BACK TO HEATH'S PLACE WASN'T AS TENSE AS HE expected. Tony neither tried again to start his conversation, nor seemed upset about waiting.

Probably meant he had an angle that he thought would bring to his side Nariko or Nana Cyr or both.

Heath didn't have time to worry about that.

Nariko had been alone with his grandmother. Was alone with her right now. Before Heath had a chance to introduce them. Before he had a chance to assess whether they'd get along or hate each other. Without even a chance to set the scene with his own choice of stories as part of the introduction.

Nariko.

Nana Cyr.

Sure. There was a chance they got along. Still...

Two opinionated women who took no shit. Both pretty damned dangerous, magically speaking.

There was a definite possibility that he would arrive to find his place on fire and the two of them fighting.

At least Dr. John was smart enough to clear out if things went that direction. Most of Heath's stuff could be replaced, but his cat?

Losing Dr. John would be a tragedy.

Still. Everything looked quiet when Tony rolled his Subaru to a stop out front.

The birds and the squirrels were both chattering, which Heath took as a good sign.

If they'd been quiet, it would have likely meant things were in a bad way. Probably.

Would have been easier to tell at night. The frogs and crickets.

Heath understood their chatter a little more naturally than the squirrels and birds.

But the current, usual-sounding chatter had to be a good sign. Didn't it?

Then again, if a fight hadn't gotten outside yet, they might not have noticed, warded up as Heath kept his place...

Smell of fresh-cut grass made Heath notice that the lawn in front of the renters had been cut. But it wasn't gardener day. If Heath lived through all this, he'd need to talk to the renters about that. No reason to see that grass cut more than the landlord wanted to pay for.

Heath shook his head. Definitely needed a nap, if he let things like that distract him. Too much tension today, and too much focus.

"Are we going in?" Tony asked, wary. His eyes kept scanning up and down the street.

"Heath?" Colin asked, studying Heath closely enough that Heath wondered just how bad he looked right now.

Heath just nodded, hoisted his backpack, and led the way.

Wards all intact. Good. Guardian spirits acting like nothing bad had happened, but they'd only care if someone were trying to get *in*...

Heath stepped a little heavier onto his front porch, to make sure he was heard inside. Rattled the doorknob just a little before opening the door—

Laughter. Honest, open laughter.

Heath found Nariko and his grandmother seated at the kitchen table over a batch of fresh-baked beignets with honey, drinking Nariko's favorite jasmine tea out of two of Heath's mismatched, thrift-store surplus mugs.

Something inside Heath relaxed.

They both turned as they heard Heath enter, and Nariko swept from her chair into his arms before he'd taken two steps.

She smelled like dirt and sweat. Days' worth of both. She wore clothes Nariko would normally never be caught dead in — canvas cargo pants and a heavy, yellow tee shirt, both even dirtier than she was. Her glittering black hair wasn't glittering right now. Been unwashed too long. Wasn't even tied in its usual bun and held in place with a single steel spike, but wound tightly behind her head and held in place with a plastic clip.

Didn't matter what she smelled like. Didn't matter what she wore. She was his Nariko, and she fit in his arms as though she'd been poured there.

Holding her was the first thing that had truly felt right all day.

Tony and Colin entered around them, and Heath could hear them talking softly to his grandmother, but he didn't care what they said.

"I missed you so much, Nari," he whispered into her ear.

"Missed you too, baby," she whispered back.

They kissed then, and Heath could have happily melted into that kiss and stayed there all weekend. In fact, only that Tony, Colin and Nana Cyr were all watching kept that kiss from going on for a good ten minutes.

When the kiss broke, Nana Cyr made a sound of approval.

"That *is* Nariko then," Colin said, voice teasing. "I mean, dressed like an office drone and rolled in dirt for ... what? At least three days?"

"Everything's a chess game for me right now," Nariko said, still holding Heath's hand as she reclaimed her seat. "Even the little details like my look and scent. Mom has all *kinds* of things out looking for me."

"Was it safe to come *here*?" Tony asked, frowning. "She'd have to have this place watched."

"Oh," Nana Cyr said casually, "probably did." She turned to Heath. "Your watchers noticed a ... what's the word? A Japanese fox spirit pacing the neighborhood. So I gave it something to look for a few blocks down. Shouldn't be back before dawn."

"*Kitsune*," Nariko said with a respectful nod. "And thank you."

"You're quite welcome, dear." Nana Cyr smiled.

"How did you know what kind of bait to use?" Colin asked.

"Didn't need to," Nana Cyr said, her tone implying that Colin should already know this. "The *kitsune* knew what it wanted to see. I just made sure it saw that, and got led on a wild ride."

Heath smiled, pleased that *he'd* known the answer. But there was something more pressing to discuss than laying tricks.

He squeezed Nariko's hand.

"What *is* the status of things with your mother?"

"That can wait," she said, her tone firm and one eyebrow high. "What's this about someone shooting at you with a *sniper rifle*?"

"A SIG Scharfschutzengewehr 3000," Tony said, "according to the waitress at Tsarina's."

"Inga'd know," Nariko said with a nod. "But that she *told* you... Just what's going on?"

Heath caught her up.

"You left something out," Tony said.

Heath sighed.

Nariko put up her hands for attention.

"Let me guess," she said. "Inga wanted something for the information. Something small, but still something you wouldn't have done."

"Something to make sure 'bored policemen' look somewhere else."

The restrained anger in Tony's voice was impressive.

"*Bored* policemen," Nariko said, raising an index finger. "Not detectives conducting an investigation."

"She's right," Heath said, keeping his tone neutral. "Could be they get harassed by bored cops who assume there's something to find."

Tony gave Heath a droll look.

"You can eyeball my boy all you want," Nana Cyr said, "but he's right. And the distinction matters. A little charm to avoid harassment, that's a fair ask for some good information. But something to throw off a formal investigation?"

Nana Cyr shook her head.

"That's a good sight more valuable."

"Reminds me," Nariko said, patting Nana Cyr's wrist. "We should talk about Heath's habit of undercharging."

"Not the time," Heath said, as much warning as he felt he could risk adding to his words.

"They are clearly criminals," Tony said. "Helping them means furthering their criminal activities."

"Far as I know," Heath said, "Tsarina's is just a restaurant. Not a way station."

"I'm sure they cook the books," Colin said. "Cash business like that?"

"And the old Russian guys," Nariko added thoughtfully. "They probably discuss business all the time. Unless they think the cops will bug it."

"My point is," Heath said, "chances are good they don't *do anything* illegal on the premises."

"I'm not sure," Tony said, "She seemed awfully concerned that I didn't try the third door, when I went to the bathroom. Could be hiding stolen goods."

Heath chuckled and shook his head. His grandmother caught the joke almost immediately.

"Oh, I *like* that," she said with a smile. "You ever open a storefront—"

"No thank you," Heath said quickly. "That is a headache I don't—"

"What's so funny?" Tony said.

"You know what's probably back there?" Heath asked with a smile. "Employee breakroom. Or maybe Inga keeps a cot back there. God knows she never seems to leave the place."

"Maybe one of the cooks is undocumented," Colin said, "and lives on site."

"But why—" Tony started, but Heath didn't need to hear the whole question.

"Made you uncomfortable, didn't it?"

Tony closed his eyes in a pained expression. "Because they didn't like me."

"Inga," Heath said to Nariko, "seems to have something against Catholic priests."

"Russian Orthodox, you think?"

"Could be atheist," Colin chimed in.

"If that room served any other purpose," Heath said, "it was obfuscation. If you're worried about the third door, then you probably never saw the trap door in the hallway."

Colin startled. "There's a—"

"Figure of speech," Nariko told him. "That aluminum floor doesn't touch the ground."

"You still helped criminals. And Inga might just have been testing the waters with you. Preparing to drag you in further."

"No," Colin said. "Heath played that part right."

Everyone seemed surprised enough by Colin's words that all eyes rounded as they turned to him.

If Colin was insulted, it didn't show.

He shrugged. "She invited him in. Offered to handle the problem for him. Heath declined. Spoke as a power in his own right. She could have pushed. She didn't. She could have negotiated for the information. She didn't. She offered the information, and suggested a small favor as a way of balancing the scales right then and there. She respects Heath's autonomy, and for a good reason."

Colin squeezed Tony's shoulder. "Heath, Nariko and me, we're good, if unsteady customers. So you better believe they've done their homework about us. They probably more know about Heath than anyone in Portland who can't get into Gripper."

"Gripper's a bar?" Nana Cyr asked Nariko, a detail that was not lost on Heath.

"You'll like it," Nariko said softly. "Practitioners only."

"You're right," Tony said suddenly, hanging his head. "I was so upset, realizing the Russian mob has a presence here in Portland, and that you guys *eat in their restaurant*, that I didn't pay enough attention to the details."

Tony drew in a sharp, deep breath and met Heath's eye.

"I agree that they're probably more interested in staying on friendly terms with you, rather than developing a business relationship." He shook his head. "I just don't like the idea of you helping criminals."

"I don't know that for sure that I did," Heath said. "Seems likely though. But to be fair, those criminals helped me first."

"What did you get besides an address and general overview?" Nariko asked.

"They've been in town about a year. Strictly small time according to Inga, but she doesn't know the magical angle."

"There was no magic today," Tony said. "Or at least, if there was, it wasn't good enough to help them out."

"Good point," Colin said. "What I saw at Flex, that was some clever work. They had to be expecting a guy like you to be charmed against random acts of violence."

"Money?" Nariko suggested. "Might be they weren't paid enough to use magic."

"Maybe," Heath said. "Or maybe it *was* a message."

"You did just meet with those others about their council idea," Tony said. "Maybe a keep-away message?"

There was a knock at the door.

"Or," Heath said with a sigh, "maybe it was all a distraction."

EVERYONE IN HEATH'S KITCHEN LOOKED AT THE DOOR, THEN AT HIM. Nariko, Nana Cyr, Tony, Colin, hell, even Dr. John looked at Heath as though to say, "Did you order us delivery?"

But that was Dr. John. His world revolved mostly around food, play, and attention.

Nice gig if you can get it.

Truth was, Heath wanted to ignore that knock.

Not just the knock, either. Maybe kick everyone out but Nariko and take a nap. He was tired enough he wouldn't even make her take a shower first, much as she might need it.

But that knock, Heath had the feeling he couldn't just ignore it.

It had been three steady, measured beats. Not the pounding of a bill collector or the timid tapping of a person in trouble.

No, there was a sense of expectation about that knock. A sense that the person on the other side of the door was someone who was used to doors opening without a knock. And when that person *did* knock, they didn't have to knock twice.

Nariko rolled her neck and shoulders. Slipped out of a pocket in her cargo pants the steel spike that usually bound her hair behind her head.

Tony reached for his crucifix, which made Heath have a wild flash on the idea that a vampire might be standing on his stoop.

He hoped not. He hadn't actually met any vampires in Portland, and he hoped to keep it that way as long as he could.

Colin reached into his back pocket for a handful of sigils he kept there. Little things he'd drawn or printed from those weird self-help books he liked so much.

Nana Cyr just raised an eyebrow at Heath.

Heath slipped his backpack off his shoulder. Took a quick sip of Nariko's jasmine tea, and swallowed as he approached the door.

Nariko took up position behind the door. The others stayed where they were. In line of sight, but not close enough to get in the way.

Of course, from their vantage points, no one would be able to see who was at the door but Heath. Not unless he threw it wide open (which would have hit Nariko).

But then, Heath didn't want any of them between him and danger anyway.

Heath picked up the tire thumper he kept by the front door. Eighteen inches of aluminum baseball bat.

Just in case.

He opened the door a crack.

Standing on the porch was a young Japanese woman who looked ... just about like Heath figured Nariko must have looked at about eighteen. She had the hair, though this girl cut hers to shoulder length, and clipped it away from her face. She had the jade eyes, though hers were a little paler.

A little slenderer though the body. Coltish. And she wore too much makeup and perfume. The makeup played with blue tones, and the perfume was something French that was supposed to be subtle.

Too much just made her smell like she'd been eating citrus in a flower bed.

But power rolled off of her in waves.

Nariko's baby sister. Kaida.

"Hello, Heath," Kaida said, as though he should have expected her. As though they were old friends, when Heath doubted they'd exchanged two dozen words in the last year. "Is my sister here?"

"Michiko?" Heath asked. "Haven't seen her in—"

"Nariko," Kaida said with a condescending smile. "You know. The one who fucks you?"

"Hey, now—"

"I can understand why," Kaida said, looking Heath over like a piece of meat. "You're positively beautiful. Not good enough to *marry* a Tachibana, of course, but certainly I could understand if she wanted to—"

"I told your mom. When Nariko left, she didn't tell me where—"

"She was going," Kaida said, practically yawning. "Yes, yes. And Mom tasted no lie in your words, though your words are harder to pick apart than most humans."

Heath felt a cold prickle down his spine at the way Kaida said "humans." Like she wasn't one of them. Yeah, Heath knew Nariko thought Kaida took after their mother, but that wasn't the same as hearing such a dismissive tone from a girl who looked so much like Nariko.

"Is she here now?"

"Tell you what," Heath said with a sigh. "If I see Nariko, I'll tell her you're looking for her."

"Is. She. Here?"

"You're awfully presumptuous for one so young."

"You're awfully rude not to invite in a guest."

"No one invited you here."

"I could come in anyway," she said with a smile.

"You could try," Heath said with an assessing nod of his head.

"But you might want to keep in mind that this is my home, where I hold *all* the aces. And I don't take well to being attacked."

"So my sister's here then. And afraid to face her little baby sister? Is that it?"

"Nariko could be here and in the shower," Heath said. "She could be off in the Rockies someplace. Doesn't matter where the fuck she is, because you're showing up here making demands, and not being very polite about it. So I don't feel any great inclination to tell you anything."

"I haven't tried to eat your house," Kaida said, as though that were somehow a reasonable thing to say.

"See, that's what I'm talking about." Heath shook his head. "Rude, saying things like that. Issuing threats. I hear from Nariko, I'll tell her you and your mother are looking for her. Best you're going to get from me."

"I suppose," Kaida said, turning away.

She turned back, trying to play as though she'd just thought of something, but she didn't have the skills to pull it off. Her turn was too quick. Rehearsed. And the words didn't flow right out of her mouth. Not to mention that her eyes never stopped smiling like she was playing some great game.

"Oh, have you seen anything of a *kitsune* named Ichiro in the neighborhood? I was supposed to meet him for a walk in Forest Park."

"Date?"

"What can I say?" She shrugged. "Not good enough to *marry* a Tachibana, but still. Have you seen him?"

"Sorry," Heath said with a bored shrug. "Haven't seen or heard from any fox spirits in days. Good luck finding him though."

She made a noncommittal sound, then her smile quirked at one side and she said something she'd clearly been looking forward to saying.

"Well, whether you talk to Nariko on the phone or whether she's in your bed right now, you tell her to get home by midnight tomorrow night. If she doesn't, well, she'll regret it for the rest of her life, however long or short that may be."

Kaida practically skipped up the driveway.

Heath closed the door. Whispered to one of his spirits to keep an eye on her, and another to let the guardians know she was to be watched for in the future.

Once he had the all-clear, he nodded at the others.

"I knew it," Nariko said with a grimace. "She's becoming an earth dragon, like Mom."

"Any chance she sensed you?"

Nariko snorted. "If she had, you'd've known. That girl has been too spoiled all her life to learn to lie."

"True," Heath said, pleased that his wards had held off the senses of a blossoming earth dragon.

"Is that what's happening tomorrow night?" Colin asked. "Some kind of dragon ascension ritual?"

Nariko looked at Colin as though he'd grown a second head.

"No," she said, shaking her head in disbelief. "There's no ritual for that. It's just ... a part of her nature that was unclear until recently. Unclear to me, anyway. Mom probably knew from birth. Might even had hidden it from me."

Heath eased her back into her chair and handed Nariko her tea, which Nana Cyr had freshly filled.

"I'd say this brings us back to you. Where do things stand?"

"I've gained a couple of important allies," Nariko said. "Mount Tabor and Rocky Butte have worked with me for years, of course, but Mom knows that. What she doesn't know is that Dixie Mountain, Cornell Mountain, and Pittock Hill all stand with me now."

"What about Council Crest and Powell Butte?" Tony asked, apparently knowing more of the local peaks by name than Heath did.

Nariko shook her head. "I could never connect with them."

"And the biggies?" Heath asked.

"Mount Saint Helens won't even talk to me. It feels some kind of kinship with Mom. As for Mount Hood..." Nariko sighed. "Only if I bring the fight there. Not willing to extend itself even as far as Multnomah Falls. Not for anyone. Not since the fire. Says all its resources are needed there."

Heath squeezed her hand, and she returned the move.

"Could I speak to your mother?" Tony asked, getting in response the most puzzled expression Heath had ever seen on Nariko's face. "Intervene, I mean. Try to prevent family violence?"

"Whatever Mom's got in mind for me," Nariko said, "I'm pretty sure she's been grooming me for it from birth. Decided that Michiko was the twin she was keeping, and I'd be the one sacrificed to her power plays."

"Murder is easier to plan, than execute. Especially when the victim is one's own child. Unless her nature is demonic and unremittingly evil—"

"Evil and good aren't really terms that apply here," Nariko said. "Not the way you mean them. This is more about ebbs and flows. Hots and colds—"

"Rada and Petro," Nana Cyr said. "Oh, I understand this, indeed I do. And I can also tell you're gearing up to tell my boy and his friends here that they should focus on him and let you deal with your family yourself."

"It would be the best way to go."

Heath opened his mouth to object, but his grandmother beat him to it.

"It would *not*," Nana Cyr said sharply. "You and Heath need each other. Don't need to spend a week around you to tell that much. You two fit together like I did with my old Remy, before he returned across the waters."

Heath barely remembered his grandfather Remy. Mostly a big bright smile and big brown eyes. But the name always felt good in Heath's ears.

"So," Nana Cyr said, standing up. "Nariko, you go take a shower and put on something fresh, even if it's Heath's. Should help you see the world a little better. Heath, you go take a nap. You look dead on your feet. Tony, Colin, I'm going to need you to run me to the store so

I can whip up a proper supper, and we can figure out how to solve *all* this ruckus."

"I made gumbo for you," Heath objected.

Nana Cyr smiled.

"Well, we'll eat that tomorrow night. Gumbo never suffers for an extra day. Now scoot!"

4

———————

Heath's bedroom didn't have a lot of furniture. Just his psychedelically painted bureau sitting under the window, and his California king bed sandwiched between a pair of octagonal night-stands, each with an incandescent reading lamp, because Heath refused to read by fluorescent light if he didn't have to.

Now was not the time for reading though. Now was the time for snoozing. Since he finally had a moment to himself.

Well, almost to himself. Dr. John was with him.

Nana Cyr, Colin and Tony, all gone to the store. Nariko naked and in Heath's shower, singing old Led Zeppelin stuff she always sang to try to calm herself down and psyche up a bit.

When Nariko sang Led Zeppelin, it meant she was scared and trying not to be. One of those little details nobody but Heath probably knew about her.

Singing Led Zeppelin, though, that would help her get over her fear, in a way Heath himself could not. Not here and now, anyway.

So Heath did the only sensible thing he could. He stretched out on his sinfully comfy, pillow-laden bed.

He was still clothed. Not even under the covers, just stretched across the dark blue comforter. Still. Dr. John was curled up and purring on his chest as though the cat had been smart enough to know all along that this nap was going to happen.

Things were bad, though. That was a simple statement of truth.

Someone wanted to kill Heath bad enough to hire hit men to do the job. Or maybe wanted to distract him. Snipers would make a hell of a good distraction...

There was a power play going on in the Portland occult community. Sure, three people were talking as though forming a council was just an idea they wanted to run past Heath. Get his opinion like they respected him. And maybe Celia did. But that Stetson Price and Tommy Wong, they'd never said a dozen words to Heath before that little lunch meeting.

Smarter to think the three of them were making a move of some sort, and trying to figure out where he stood.

Might mean one or more of them were behind that sniper. Oh, not directly. Not with the promises they'd made. Breaking those kinds of promises, that would be the kind of thing that could come back to bite a practitioner in the ass.

Spirits find out you don't keep your word, and suddenly their own word means less to them, when they're dealing with you.

Still. That didn't mean there weren't ways *around* darn near any promise. And maybe Stetson Price didn't seem to be the sharpest cheese in the drawer. But that Tommy Wong and Celia Martinez, though, they were clever enough to get crafty...

Could also be that someone wanted to spook Heath away from them. Could be he'd show up at Gripper tonight or tomorrow — whenever really — and find out someone took pot shots at them too.

Maybe.

Then there was Nariko's mother and sister. They had to fit into all of this somewhere...

Somewhere...

But sleep, it tugged at Heath. Buoyed as it was by the purring, contented cat on his chest, and the comforting presence of Nariko in his shower.

She was singing Black Sabbath now. At least, Heath *thought* that song was by Black Sabbath. Something about fools and mob rule and that kind of thing.

That was a good sign. And good signs, they just made Heath more comfortable. Settled him in a little more...

And then he was drifting.

Not quite off into slumberland. Not quite off into the place between either, though it wouldn't have surprised Heath to end up there. He'd been ending up there in dreams more than he liked, lately.

Then again, once in a decade was more than Heath would have liked, when it came to the place between.

But Heath wasn't quite awake either, as he lay there drifting. He lost track of the sound of Nariko showering. The sound of her singing. He even lost track of Dr. John's purr, and a loud rumble like that, right in the middle of his chest, wasn't exactly an easy thing to ignore.

Instead, Heath floated in that languorous state between sleep and wakefulness. That state where everything's dark, but a comfortable kind of dark. A warm place he could just sink into and not think about anything for a little while until sleep finally took him.

But something else got there first.

Laughter.

Wasn't low or menacing, which was a plus. But it was familiar, that laughter. Had a bit of a nasal quality, but that wasn't quite helping Heath place it the way it should have.

In fact, it wasn't until the laughter stopped and the voice started to talk that Heath realized who it was.

"Well, seems to me you've gone and gotten yourself stuck again."

Ghede Brav. Owner of the tin flask that Heath kept tucked away in his kitchen.

Now, Heath would have been willing to swear that he only *thought* his response to that implied query from Brav, but he still heard it in his ears as though he'd spoken it aloud.

"Stuck a couple of ways, I think. Which one did you have in mind?"

More laughter. And a secondary laughter sound too, as of two or three of Brav's smoky skulls, echoing the thoughts of the Ghede.

"Really? Are you asking which of your various problems *I* consider the most important?"

Heath didn't really see or feel himself nod, but apparently the idea got across.

"Well," Brav said, drawing the word out to at least three syllables. "Maybe you learned a little something from our last talk?"

"Maybe not, since it seems I'm stuck again."

Laughter, and enough echoes now that Heath could almost — *almost* — picture Brav. Dressed in mottled funeral attire. Too thin and skin darker even than Heath's father, except when, from certain angles, Brav looked cadaverous.

And the echoes were the smoky skulls generated by Brav's cigar. At least five of them, likely floating around his head even now.

"You, my boy..." Brav gave this sense of considering Heath. Looking him up and down. "You aren't going to debate me on that point, are you? That you are my boy?"

Now, Heath knew full well that Brav was intending that sentence two ways. The first was the implication that Brav might be his father, but that was just the kind of sex joke Ghedes liked to tell. If Heath had addressed that part, Brav would have laughed and told Heath to ask his mother.

Instead Heath addressed the second point.

"I understand that I'm *kanzo*, so I don't dispute that or the connection it gives me to the Lwa."

"Well, well, aren't you generous. Maybe if those britches have gotten too tight, you don't need any advice from the likes of me."

"I didn't mean that at all," Heath said quickly. "It was just a shock to realize."

Laughter. That was a good sign, even if it did carry more than a hint of mockery.

"Too sure of yourself and your reality, my boy. Need to realize ain't but one thing set in stone."

"The grave?"

"Well, I was thinking of your tombstone, but that'll do."

Heath wasn't sure what to say to that, but Brav kept talking.

"So what I had in mind about you being stuck…

Brav seemed somehow to lean closer. The next words that Heath couldn't so much hear as sense, felt as though they were whispered in his ear by breath that smelled of spiced rum, cigars, and decay.

"You've let them make you a fulcrum, boy."

"Who?"

"Lots of answers to that question. Better question is…"

"What can I do about it?"

"That's my boy." Laughter then, followed by words with laughter still in Brav's voice. *"A man was stuck in a rut. / He was hard, but just couldn't nut. / A girl offered help / and then gave a yelp. / For now he's stuck in her butt."*

"Sounds like someone needed lube," Heath said.

"Doesn't it just?"

"But if I'm the fulcrum, then what's…"

"Heath?"

That last was Nariko's voice. And that warmth had to be her hand on his shoulder.

Heath woke with the sound of laughter fading in his ears.

FAR AS HEATH WAS CONCERNED, THE BEST POSSIBLE SIGHT TO WAKE UP to was a naked Nariko, warm from the shower and saying his name softly.

The second best sight, though, had to be Nariko, warm from the shower and saying his name softly, dressed only in *his* shirt.

Right now, her hair was loose and glittering again, hanging down past her shoulders. She appeared to be wearing nothing more than one of his button-up shirts. Short-sleeved and green-and-white striped, it hung just long enough to get interesting if she did more than stand there.

Of course, it wasn't buttoned up all the way either, so as she leaned over him where he lay on the bed, the view that direction was pretty fine as well.

Yes, there was still the little detail that he himself remained fully dressed, but that could be taken care of easily enough.

Naturally, he pulled her down to join him.

As the bedsprings announced her arrival, Nariko gave an adorable yip of surprise before she started laughing.

Dr. John, who *had been* snoozing away quite happily on Heath's chest, took off in a huff. But that was just as well, all things considered, even if his claws left marks of their displeasure behind them.

Heath pulled Nariko close. Gazed deeply into her smiling, jade green eyes. Stroked gentle fingertips across her cheek, still warm and soft from the shower. Breathed deep to savor the scents of her. The clean smell that was all her, underneath the subtle hints of jasmine perfume she must have dabbed on.

"Five minutes, you two!" Nana Cyr's voice, calling down the hall and carrying through the closed door of his bedroom.

In the moment of silence following that knell of doom, Heath could hear his other guests in the kitchen. Soft voices, dishes, and the sharp complaints of rudeness by one put-out Dr. John.

How Dr. John had made his escape through a closed door was just one of the mysteries of that cat.

A mystery that could wait.

"Long as I've been away from you," Nariko said, her voice as soft and tempting as her skin while she burrowed fingers under his shirt, "five minutes might be enough. If we're quick..."

Heath growled low in his throat — a sound he knew she loved — but forced a deep breath through his nose.

"But if it isn't, that wouldn't be fair to you. And this would *not* be the time to keep my grandmother waiting."

"I suppose not," Nariko said, then sighed heavily. She started to pull away, but Heath pulled her back down tight.

That got him an inquisitive eyebrow.

"Just because we have to wait for *that* doesn't mean I don't get to hold you."

That got him a happy sigh as Nariko snuggled down to wrap herself around him.

Heath's trailing hand down her waist quickly discovered that she was indeed naked under his shirt, which made him pull that hand right up to her hip immediately.

After all, he could withstand only so much temptation.

Nariko chuckled.

"Of all the times," she lamented.

Heath just nodded, his chin moving against her soft hair.

"You owe me," she said, tapping fingers along his sternum.

"You're the one who went out of town."

"But you weren't immediately available on my return," she said, as though that were the most obvious offense in the world.

"I see," Heath said, smiling. "And I'm just supposed to be perpetually available to you?"

"That's right." She kissed him on the collarbone. "I thought I'd made that clear."

"You've been hanging out with Dr. John too much."

"He has some interesting ideas," Nariko teased. "I'm thinking of subscribing to his newsletter."

A gentle rapping on the door. A cleared throat.

"I'm … erm…" Tony sounded uncomfortable enough that Heath wanted to laugh. He was pretty sure Nariko could feel him resisting, through little twitches along his rib cage. "I'm supposed to remind you both to be getting dressed."

"No rest for the wicked," Heath said.

"But I didn't get to do anything *wicked*," Nariko protested.

"Thank you, Tony," Heath called out loud. "We'll be out in a sec."

No response. Probably already fled back down the hall.

"At least she didn't send Colin," Heath said. "He'd've tried to come *in* and tell us."

"Yeah," Nariko said, sighing as she sat up, "and he'd be as disappointed as I am that you're wearing clothes."

"Makes three of us, believe me," Heath said, sitting up and

stretching. "Given my druthers, I'd keep you in this bed all weekend, and let the rest of the world just wait."

Nariko turned and gave Heath a look he wasn't used to. It was a little more serious, from the way her jaw was set, but still soft around the eyes.

And there was something more there. Something he couldn't quite put his finger on.

"I'm going to hold you to that," she said softly. "We survive the next few days first. But then, for a few days, it's just us. You, me, and Dr. John, and we don't leave this bedroom to go any farther than your kitchen."

"It's a promise," Heath said.

Nariko grabbed him by the face and kissed him then. Hard and deep and so passionate it felt like she was personally turbo charging every inch of him, toes to nose.

When she pulled back, her breathing was even more ragged than his, her pupils wild and cheeks flushed. But she turned and slipped into underwear — her own — and picked up a pair of black yoga pants she must have left here at some point without his even realizing.

Heath had to stand up and straighten his own clothes. Turn away from the sight and smell of her getting ready to leave the room.

As he did, he heard the distant echoes of Ghede Brav's voice.

"Lots of ways to be stuck, little fool. And some of them aren't so bad..."

***

When Heath and Nariko, each with an arm around the other, started down the hardwood floor of his hall toward the kitchen, the wonderful smells of his grandmother's cooking were almost enough to make leaving the bedroom worthwhile.

Almost.

Not three steps down the hall, Nariko said, "What is that heavenly smell?"

Heath sighed happily. "Shrimp etouffee."

His mouth watered at the blend of peppers, onions, paprika and more, so much more. All whipped together in a roux that Heath knew would make every single one of his taste buds want to come shake his grandmother's hand.

"Can you make that?" Nariko asked.

"Yes," Heath admitted, "but not as well as she can."

"If it's half as good, I may have to marry you."

Heath gave her a squeeze.

When they reached his sunny kitchen, the table was already set. And Heath's little kitchen table wasn't designed for all the place settings it held, but somehow it worked.

Tony and Colin had dug out Heath's folding chairs to make sure there was enough seating, and made placemats out of paper towels.

Probably the first time that those sea green dishes Nariko had bought Heath — she'd let Heath keep his mugs, but refused to live with the rest of his mismatched thrift store castoff dishes — saw use the way their designers had intended.

Still. Five people at that little table?

They'd all be in each other's way. Just like the family reunions Heath could barely remember from his early childhood, down in New Orleans.

Just added to the hominess of the feel, along with the cooking warmth in the kitchen.

Then Heath saw the counter.

"Just how many meals were you planning to make?" Heath asked.

Darn near every inch of his countertops was covered in food. Vegetables, meats, and it looked as though his grandmother'd bought the ingredients to do more than a little baking as well.

Nana Cyr just smiled and said, "you only have enough gumbo for one meal, the way this one eats," and she slapped Colin's surprisingly flat belly.

Colin grinned like he'd hit the lottery.

Which he might have. Heath was never quite sure where Colin got his money, only that he had a lot of it.

"Oh," Nana Cyr said, over her shoulder. "I whipped you up a little something in the other room, too. Should help if anyone else shoots at you. You'll know where to find it."

Heath did. She'd likely tucked it behind a book at the right end of the third shelf, probably of his righthand bookcase. That'd be symmetrical with where she used to hide conjure hands for him, back in New York.

That wasn't a parental approval or disapproval thing. Heath's dad never took up the path, but he never hesitated to ask his mother for a little rootwork now and again, so he certainly wouldn't have object to his son getting a little help too, from time to time.

And Heath's mother, well, she had her own thing going, but Heath didn't know much about it. He did know that she and his grandmother seemed to respect each other.

No, little rootwork presents Heath's grandmother left for him were hidden away for an entirely different reason.

Mojo bags, conjure hands ... whatever you called them, only two people were ever supposed to see them, let alone touch them — the person who made them, and the person who used them. Even Nariko didn't get to see the ones he made for...

Wait.

Nana Cyr had been shopping, cooking *and* conjuring? Not to mention cleaning up Heath's worktable too, and probably putting everything back right where Heath would have put it himself...

"Just how long was my nap?" Heath asked Nariko.

She shrugged. "I know I ran you out of hot water. I hadn't had a good shower in too long."

Nana Cyr was smiling as she turned to Heath, but then stopped in her tracks with sudden thunder to the movement. It was as though a tornado had been whipping through the area, then stopped just short of one house, and sat there. Like it was still considering picking that house up and flinging it across the state lines.

That was how Nana Cyr looked at Heath.

Then she narrowed her eyes and looked closer. Heath knew better than to question her, or even move much, but he felt himself pulling his shoulders in, as though he were guilty. Though he couldn't imagine what he might be guilty *of*.

Nana Cyr shook her head, like she'd decided he *was* guilty.

She stepped right up to Heath and sniffed him, just under the chin. A move that actually made Nariko blush, even though she and Heath hadn't been doing anything ... smelly.

Colin and Tony must have frozen solid, they stood so still over by the counters.

"Heath," Nana Cyr said in an arch tone, "just *whose* cigar am I smelling?"

"Cigar?" Nariko said, frowning in puzzlement. "I don't smell any cigar."

"Ghede Brav," Heath said through a sigh. "While I was napping. Sort of. Not really sleeping, but—"

"Weren't in the place between, were you?" Nana Cyr said, still right in close.

"No, ma'am," Heath said. "I was just floating, when he started talking to me."

"Does that a lot, does he?"

"No, ma'am," Heath was starting to resent feeling like he was on trial when he hadn't done anything wrong. But he couldn't stop himself from feeling like he was sixteen again and caught out after curfew while his parents were out of town.

Nana Cyr kept one eyebrow so high, it might have been the sword of Damocles ready to fall on him.

"You know why he can do that, right? Just talk to you any old time he wants, if you happen to be in the right frame of mind? Or near enough to it, anyway?"

"I have his flask." Even those words sounded guilty, coming out of Heath's mouth.

"No," she said, shaking her head slowly. "It's 'cause you've been keeping your head too open. Oh, the flask might've been his way in, but he's only making himself at home because you let him."

Heath's turn to arch an eyebrow. "And just how was I supposed to know I could do anything about it? Seeing as I didn't know I was *kanzo* until today?"

If Nana Cyr felt any guilt about the lateness of that revelation, it sure didn't show. She just shook her head slowly, holding onto his eyes.

"And I suppose," she said, "that you couldn't have called me to ask about it? Or maybe even asked some local *manbo* about the situation?"

"One," Heath said, starting to feel and sound a little more adult now, largely because the second point he had to raise was getting him back onto more familiar turf. "I don't go running to my grandmother with every little problem I run across."

"And Ghede Brav is a little problem?"

"The flask is a little problem, and I thought Brav's continued presence was more about that than about me."

Nana Cyr pondered that for a moment, then gave a slow nod. "And what's two?"

"Two," Heath said, "is that I don't have anything to do with any of the local *humfos*. Not those led *manbos*, nor those led by *houngans*. Not any of the local *bokors*, either. Didn't want to give anyone the impression that I was looking to sign up, and coming to them with a problem would give them leverage when it comes to other clients. Which you should know, Nana."

Nana Cyr frowned. She did know. She just always felt that Hoodoo, even done right, needed to properly be done with the aid of the Lwa, which meant — in her mind — someone at least qualified to run a *humfo*, even if they didn't do it.

"All right," she said, easing back down and returning to her cooking.

The whole room seemed to breathe again. Or maybe it was just Colin and Tony, both doing so noisily for a moment.

Nariko looked as though she'd never even thought of blushing. What was more, she stood beside Heath as though he might need her support in dealing with his grandmother.

Wow. Everything Nariko was going through personally, and she was willing to stand against *Nana Cyr* if need be?

She must really love Heath.

He slipped an arm around her waist, while Nana Cyr finished off the etouffee and asked the most important question over her shoulder.

At least, the most important question on the Brav front.

"So, what did he have to say, while you were napping?"

"He laughed mostly. Said I was stuck again. And also said I'd let them make me a—"

Heath's phone rang.

"A what?" Nana Cyr said, but the number belonged to Celia Martinez.

"One sec, Nana. I have to take this."

ALMOST EVERYONE IN THE KITCHEN TURNED TO LOOK AT HEATH. His grandmother, with her eyebrows high. Tony, with as little expression as he could manage but still conveying surprise. Colin, not trying to hide his surprise at all. Nariko, looking ready to fight whoever was on the phone.

In fact, apparently Nariko had managed to pull out her steel hair spike and bind her hair back in a bun. The way she did when things got serious, but not yet ready to come to blows.

When had she done that?

The only one in the kitchen not looking at Heath was Dr. John, who had gotten Nana Cyr to give him some shrimp, and was eating them slowly, savoring them.

Heath stepped away from the delightful aroma of his grandmother's shrimp etouffee and along the hardwood floor into the fresh smells of his recently cleaned living room.

He ran one hand along his worktable while he answered the call from Celia Martinez.

"Didn't know you had my number," he said as he answered.

"Was I not supposed to?" Celia asked, but not like it was a question. About what he expected her to say. He would have said something similar himself, in the same situation. A way of acknowledging the comment, without saying how she'd come by the number, when, and so forth.

It was the kind of talking-without-meaningful-information that all good rootworkers figured out how to do somewhere along the lines. It was a game of sorts. A little disinformation, a little misinformation, and a lot of giving people a chance to give things away without knowing they'd done it.

Already, Heath felt as though he was working, not talking. Was that the point?

"So, it's your dime," he said.

"I'm glad to hear your voice. To know you're up and about. I ... wasn't sure it would even be you answering your phone."

"No? Why? What have you heard?"

Pretty direct question, but then, she'd set him up for it well enough.

"Well..."

While she considered her words, Heath could hear what sounded like the voices of children in the background. Children speaking Spanish, if he wasn't mistaken. Meant she was likely calling from home. Maybe even her kitchen. But was that good or bad? And was it even the actual situation? Or was she calling from somewhere that would *sound* like she was just calling from her kitchen?

Just more things to ponder, while she spoke again.

"Word got around that, after the meeting, someone had tried to take your life. Fired shots at you, using a rifle of some sort. The rest of what people are saying, that is little less certain."

"How so?"

More hesitation. Heath was pretty sure he could hear something bubbling. A stove then?

No alerts from his guardians, though. That had to be a good thing, at least...

"Some have been saying ... some have been saying you were hit.

Wounded badly and taken to a ... well, the phrase I heard was 'clandestine location, condition unknown.' But that ... that was from an idiot trying to sound like a newscaster."

"Listen to idiots a lot, do you?"

"I did have better information that said you had survived. But ... my sources were quiet about what really happened. Where you were. Whether you were in good shape, or at death's door." She sighed, and Celia was the kind of woman who made her sighs *heavy*. "I was worried."

She'd said her "sources" were quiet. So she'd had some spirits of her own checking into Heath's condition, and they couldn't get to him to gather any useful information.

Interesting.

"Worried about me? Or about yourself?"

"Heath," she said, trying for an admonishing tone. It wasn't bad, but she had nothing on Nana Cyr. "You can't possibly think I had anything to do with it."

"Anything to do with what?"

"Whoever was stupid enough to shoot at you with a rifle, of course. What else could I have meant?"

Heath shrugged. No, it wouldn't carry through the phone lines, but that didn't matter. Far as Heath was concerned, Celia could hear the pause and read into it whatever she wanted. He was far enough from the kitchen now that she wouldn't be able to hear the others filling their plates with food and their glasses with water.

Of course, all of Heath's guests were moving like mice, paying at least as much attention to his conversation as they were to putting dinner on the table.

"Celia," Heath said, "all I know for sure is that I came to a meeting with you three. A meeting some might call 'clandestine.' I mean, it wasn't at Gripper, was it?"

"You know why we wanted to meet there."

"I know what you told me," Heath said, letting his tone stay neutral so she could hear the words however she wanted. They'd sound *really bad* if she felt guilty about anything. "I also don't have any reason to think you told anyone about that meeting but me. Which reduces the number of people who knew I'd be there today."

"Well—"

"I *also* know I turned down your offer. Turned it down flat. No mistaking. No 'I'll think about it' crap. Flat no."

Heath gave a quick sigh, and continued before Celia could respond.

"Then I left the restaurant, walked maybe a couple hundred feet, and someone tried to forcefully increase my lead content."

"Heath," Celia said. Almost sounded worried now. Heath didn't believe it, but he let her talk. "Heath, you heard the vows we swore at the table."

"I assure you, I heard every word that the three of you said through the whole meeting. Going to pretend there's no way to get around an oath? I mean, if you want me to start listing ways it could be done—"

"I had nothing to do with it."

"So you know who did then?"

"No!"

"But you just said *you* had nothing to do with it. What about your cronies? Maybe the one stupid enough to try to sound like a newscaster when bragging about taking me out?"

"Stetson? He's not the one I made the newscaster crack about. That was ... a man you don't know."

"Sound pretty sure there. Portland's a small town..."

"*I know I had nothing to do with it,*" she insisted, still not identifying the would-be newscaster, which Heath found interesting. "And I'm *sure* Stetson and Tommy didn't either."

"Didn't what?" Heath asked. "Pull the trigger? Oh, I don't doubt that none of the three of you actually pulled the trigger."

"Heath, I'm saying *none* of us had anything to do with any attempt on your life today."

Heath noted she wasn't disavowing any past or future attempts on his life, but that was a topic that could — hopefully — wait for later.

"Willing to swear to that? On your spirits? Maybe even on your power?"

Yep. Definitely water boiling in the background, on the other end of the line. And Heath could hear a young woman trying to wrangle those children.

Of Celia, he didn't even hear any breathing.

"Didn't think so," he said.

"You can't honestly expect me to swear anything like that. Not to guarantee the behavior of others."

Sounded defeated now. Even more interesting.

"No? Don't trust your cronies that far? See, *I* trust *my* friends that far. Watch. I swear on my power that none of the following people have made any attempts on your life so far today: me, Brother Tony, Weird Colin Driscoll, and Nariko Tachibana."

"Heath—"

"Now, if you wanted me to swear against *future* attempts, well, that would be shortsighted of me right now, wouldn't it?"

"What are you saying?"

Was that fear he heard in her voice? He certainly hoped so.

"All I'm saying is that if I find whoever tried to kill me today *and* find proof that you and your cronies weren't involved, then you and I have no beef. But if I don't... For that matter, if I find proof that anyone *associated* with you three had any hand in it. Well, then let's just say you might want to up your life insurance. For your kids' sakes."

"I see," she said, and Heath was pretty sure he heard her swallow in there too.

"So," Heath said, "one might even think it's in your own best interests to find proof of your innocence. Given that a misunderstanding, from my position, would be pretty easy to understand."

"I see," she said again, a little more thoughtful this time. "This your way of trying to get help finding out who tried to kill you?"

"Nope," Heath said with so much direct honesty that Celia couldn't have helped but hear it. "I'm just saying that I'm going to find out who tried to kill me. And I'm going to take care of it. And if what I find doesn't clear you three, then you are in no way above suspicion."

"A lot to put on our heads, just on coincidence," Celia said, her tone neutral. "After all, even if *we* didn't tell anyone where you'd be, *you* told people. I know Father Antonio was spotted at the café across the street, during the meeting. Seems like an unlikely coincidence to me."

"Difference is," Heath said, "I know I can trust my friends not to blab to anyone who might try to kill me." He shook his head. "Don't know that I can trust you three."

"But—"

"Come on, Celia," Heath said, tone frank. "You were in my shoes, what would *you* think?"

She thought about that through one long, slow breath.

"I didn't have anything to do with it. I'll swear to that, if you want."

"Not enough," Heath said, noting she didn't just swear right there and then. Only offered to do it. Which meant she wasn't as certain of her allies as she pretended, since "anything to do with it" would include setting him up, even unknowingly.

After all, one could be held accountable for the actions of one's allies. At least, when those allies might have been trying to take Heath's life.

"There's nothing I can say here and now, then, is there? To make you believe I had nothing to do with it?"

"Best you can do is look into it yourself. Take a little responsibility for putting me in the firing line, even if it turns out you didn't know the attempt was coming."

She started to say something, but Heath spoke over her.

"Barring that, the second best thing you can do is nothing. Just hold tight and wait, and see what I find out. If you're really so sure of your boys, then that's all you really need to do anyway. And I'm sure you've got better ways to spend your time."

"If you find proof that I'm innocent," she said, "will I get an apology?"

"Depends," Heath said. "Can you tell me here and now that you think my suspicions are unreasonable? Not whether or not they're *merited*, but are they *unreasonable*?"

She sighed, long and slow and heavy.

"No," she said. "I'd think the same thing, if I were you."

"Don't think there'll be an apology then." He shrugged. "Tell you what, though. I find out for sure that you weren't involved, I'll at least tell you."

"Thank you for that. At least."

"Bye, Celia."

He let her say goodbye, protesting her innocence one more time, before he clicked off.

He turned around to see everyone sitting at his kitchen table. Too many people for that small table, but it looked right somehow. Comfortable.

Of course, they were all looking at him with different expressions.

Colin with a little awe, as though he couldn't believe Heath had spoken to Celia Martinez that way.

Tony with a bit of a frown, though Heath couldn't tell whether that was because Tony disapproved of Heath's accusation or because he disapproved of Heath telling a potential killer she was under suspicion.

Nariko was smiling fondly. She liked hearing Heath talk tough. Didn't happen all that often.

Nana Cyr was smiling with approval. It was funny to Heath, though, thinking about it. It wasn't his grandmother who'd taught him not to back down from a fight that came to him.

It was Heath's mother.

No business at the dinner table. That was an old rule in the Cyr family. Heath could even remember cousins visiting, back in New Orleans when he was a kid.

Didn't matter the reason for the visit. Didn't matter if some business matter was pressing and had to get resolved before midnight, which seemed to happen more often than it should have, when Heath thought back on it.

After all, how many business deals got conducted outside of normal business hours, much less had expirations set at a time like midnight?

Then again, Heath had never worked in the corporate sector. Not that many of his Louisiana relatives did either. They'd mostly worked in service and retail. Owned little gas stations, stores, that kind of thing, here and there around Louisiana. Of course, those businesses didn't seem to Heath to conduct a lot of business close to midnight either...

Anyway, no matter how things were pressing on Heath and company as they sat around his little kitchen table, the only conversation allowed had to be purely social.

And Nana Cyr took shameless advantage of that as they began eating.

She got Nariko talking about her college education (Business Master's in Negotiation, which Heath figured the whole western world had to have figured out by now), and about her hobbies. Though she'd only really gotten to talk about riding her motorcycle before Colin burst in, needing to talk some himself.

Colin talked about his music, mostly, but Nana Cyr wanted to hear all about that too. Even told a few stories of her own, singing in the jazz clubs around New Orleans. Shows she'd done with Professor Longhair, Dr. John (the musician, not the cat), and other names Heath wasn't used to hearing around Portland all that often.

Nana Cyr even let the conversation wander then, likely so Nariko didn't feel as though she were getting the third degree from the matriarch of Heath's family.

Tony told a couple of amusing monk anecdotes, which were a thing Heath hadn't realized existed.

Apparently funny things happened in monasteries sometimes, same as they did anywhere else. Especially since the monks of the Protective Order of Saint Benedict loved their beer.

In fact, it might have been the only concession to business that no one seemed to expect Heath to talk during dinner. They were all happy enough to go on a bit themselves, and just let him relax. Maybe even do a little thinking.

And Heath didn't mind that a bit.

As a matter of fact, by the time they'd finished that wonderful, spicy shrimp etouffee along with the soft, chewy rye bread that Nana Cyr had somehow found time to bake, Heath had a pretty good idea of what he wanted to do.

Of course, telling the others about that got interrupted by fresh king cake.

King cake, that was something Heath hadn't even had when he lived in New York, let alone out here on the West Coast. No, king cake was something he barely remembered from childhood Mardi Gras days back in New Orleans.

A good king cake was like a giant cinnamon roll baked in heaven, frosted in gold, purple and green, and covered in sprinkles.

During Mardi Gras there'd be a little plastic baby Jesus in the middle, as a blessing. Heath doubted Nana Cyr had managed to dig one of those up, though.

Still...

"Where did you find the time to do all this?" Heath asked as Nana Cyr set the king cake in the middle of the table.

"Never could do just one thing at a time," she said.

Colin's hand darted out, but Nana Cyr smacked it.

"You'll get the same size slice as everyone else, Mr. Greedy," she said, but Colin didn't look abashed. He still looked as though he was enjoying the best meal of his life.

Light as mist, that cake was. The frosting had a sweet taste that seemed to prepare the mouth for what was to come. Then the cinnamon zinged in with a pop that got all your attention, then slowly eased back until it lingered just enough to make sure you knew you might never taste anything better, but every dessert would get compared to it.

As Heath finished his slice, he decided that if this had been his last meal, it would have been the right choice.

But then the cake was eaten and more coffee was poured, and everyone was looking at Heath. Tony was the first to speak.

"Do you really think Celia Martinez, Tommy Wong, and Stetson Price were behind the gunman?"

"I wouldn't feel confident saying they weren't."

"Better question is," Nana Cyr said, "what are we going to do about it?"

"Let me run down some contacts of my own," Tony said. "I can come at this from an angle ... none of you can."

Now, there was a chance that Tony was talking about resources his order gave him access too. But Heath suspected he had something more in mind than that. Made Heath wonder, and not for the first time, just what exactly Tony had done before he became a monk...

"What can I do?" Colin asked.

"Still got those invisibility spells of yours?" Heath asked. He knew the answer, of course, but he knew Colin would enjoy answering the question.

Because Colin didn't just have some variation of *ignore-me* charm. No, what he'd dug up in one of his weird self-help books was the real deal. As in, anyone could look right at Colin and not see him.

Colin was the only person Heath had ever met who could really pull that off, and every time Heath saw him do it — so to speak — Colin implied he could do a whole lot more.

"'Course," Colin said, letting his tone and his smile do his implying for him. "I only break out the invisibility for a special occasion, but I'd say this qualifies."

"Feel up to breaking into Flex?"

"On his own?" Tony objected.

"I was going to ask you to watch his back, but—"

"Wait," Tony said, even raising a hand to emphasize his point. He turned to Colin. "That invisibility thing—"

"I'd trust it anywhere, anytime."

Not even a hint of playfulness in Colin's tone. Nana Cyr raised an eyebrow, but Nariko nodded that Colin was right.

Anything that could slip past Nariko could probably slip past the gates of Hell, if need be.

"All right then," Tony said, "you come with me. Stay invisible, stay quiet, and keep what happens to yourself. Then we'll go to Flex afterwards."

Colin rubbed his hands together eagerly.

"What about us?" Nariko asked.

"I hope you're including *me* in that 'us,'" Nana Cyr said, and Nariko gave her a nod and a smile.

"We're going to do what I promised you earlier, Nana," Heath said with a smile. "We're going to show you Gripper."

5

Tony and Colin would be leaving Heath's house first, after the dishes were in the dishwasher and the kitchen cleaned up.

Neither activity took long, and soon the two of them were headed for the door. Colin looking eager as a puppy getting a trip to the park. Tony, looking ... not just serious.

No. Tony looked dangerous. In a way Heath wasn't used to seeing him. It was as though, wherever he was going and whatever he was about to do, brought back old habits in ways that might not be good for the monk. Changed his posture, his body language, his expression.

He was still dressed like a monk. Head to toe back wool. But he carried himself like something a lot less holy.

Tony got as far as Heath's front door before Heath said, "Stop."

Even the way Tony turned his head had changed. There was a dark fire in his eyes that Heath had never seen before. He didn't look curious that Heath had spoken, but irritated at the interruption.

"Don't do this," Heath said, shaking his head. "Not if you have to go back to something that makes you..." Heath gestured to Tony, up and down. "...like that. Like maybe what you left behind isn't so far behind as you think."

Tony shook his head, and a tremor followed the movement right down his body.

Just like that, Tony looked like, well, Tony. *Brother* Tony, to be specific.

"Thank you for that," Tony said, sounding more like himself. "But I assure you. The old ways no longer tempt me. It's part of our training, to ensure that we take only those whose lives are now truly dedicated to the calling. No monk of my order is allowed to take his or her vows until a tribunal is satisfied."

He shook his head. "People throw the phrase 'devil's advocate' around, but I assure you. It has a real meaning in my circles. And the associated investigation is ... intensive. They have no doubts about me, and neither should you."

"But—"

"If I'm going to get ... these people to take me seriously, they must believe me. I know how to convince them. That is all I'm doing."

Heath frowned, uncertain.

"I promise," Tony said firmly.

"Then thank you again," Heath said, and the changes came over Tony's posture like he was putting on his coat. This time, even Colin seemed to notice, with a weirded-out expression.

Something to see on that boy's face.

They left then, and Heath was just turning to his girlfriend and grandmother when—

"Fuck!" Nariko swore, shaking her head. Still drying her hands on a dishtowel.

Nana Cyr turned surprised eyes on Nariko, but Heath suspected he knew why she swore.

Nariko didn't leave any question in his mind.

"Colin and Tony just left. Together."

"That's right," Heath said, letting her get to her point in her time.

"I don't suppose you'd let me page a ride share."

"Not with some unknown person gunning for me."

"So public transit is out for the same reason."

Heath nodded, unapologetic.

"So you *do* plan to drive."

"Not my favorite way to get around, but it does seem the best method, under the circumstances."

"Why is this a problem?" Nana Cyr asked.

"Nari doesn't like my car."

"That piece of shit rust bucket doesn't deserve to be *called* a car," Nariko corrected him. "And I refuse to be seen in it."

"Half the point of taking my car is that we *won't* be seen."

Nariko tossed down her dishtowel with an air of finality.

"The car is that bad?"

"No," Heath said, in the same moment that Nariko said, *"Yes."*

"So you're not coming?" Nana Cyr asked.

"Oh, I'm coming," Nariko said. "But I'll take my bike, thank you very much. And I better put on business clothes."

She started walking back down the hall toward Heath's room.

Nana Cyr gave Heath a questioning look.

"It's not that bad. The *Parakeet* is perfect for what I need from a car, and it's more reliable than just about anything else on the road."

"Hah," Nariko said, walking back up the hall in black leather pants and a form-fitting shirt the color of dark caramel.

All of it was clean, which was good. And Heath remembered when both articles of clothing *entered* his house, which was even better.

As for the speed at which she'd changed, well, he'd gotten used to that. When she wasn't teasing him with her body, Nariko had the kind of quick-change skills that suggested she'd done some modeling that she hadn't admitted to.

Still. Heath found himself lamenting that she was *leaving* his bedroom, looking like that.

Alas, though, there was work to be done.

She did, at least, give him a kiss goodbye before making her way out the door.

"You've got it bad," Nana Cyr said with a smile, once the door was closed. "Good thing she's got it just as bad for you."

"Here's hoping it stays that way," Heath said. "Things haven't always been smooth between us."

"Past is past," Nana Cyr said, standing up and picking up her purse. "Now, let's see about this rust bucket of yours."

In short order, she was standing over Heath's car. And from the sigh she let out, she was hardly giving it the look of approval.

Heath's car had started life as a red, AMC Gremlin hatchback. A car that had likely been old when Heath was born. And when he was honest with himself, Heath admitted that he was surprised the car had lived long enough to come into his possession.

Wasn't so much red these days. Heath still liked to think it was on the red side of brown, but it still looked a little more like old blood than he liked.

Wouldn't paint it, though. Wouldn't change a thing about how it looked.

No, the look was all part of what Heath wanted from this car. It was *supposed* to look like a hunk of junk.

Made everything Heath had done to it easier. Well, most of it, anyway. The parts that mattered most that day.

Without even an ounce of rootwork on Heath's part, he had here a car that other drivers — and pedestrians, for that matter — did their level best to ignore. To keep away from. To give a wide berth to. Because anything that ancient and beat up could only be driven by a driver who wouldn't hesitate to smack a bumper he didn't like.

Cops *started* with the assumption that the car couldn't reach, let alone surpass, any reasonable speed limit.

By the time Heath had finished laying tricks on that car, it was charmed against tickets, thieves, accidents, damn near any kind of hazard that could befall it. Observers would have trouble noticing it as anything except space to be avoided, and they'd forget it just as soon as they could.

And with all that taken care of, Heath had thrown in a bunch of other little upgrades...

Yes, in Heath's mind, the *Parakeet* was a fine, fine automobile.

"Think it's too late to catch a ride on the back of your girlfriend's bike?" Nana Cyr asked.

Heath turned his head slowly to look at her. Blinked just as slow.

"I can call her back for you, if you like," he said, voice neutral.

She broke into a wide smile. "Just teasing. You did good. Started with the right kind of base for your needs, and just conjured the rest."

Heath smiled wide and felt his heart lurch ahead at his grandmother's blatant approval. He opened the door with a grand gesture.

She took her seat. Settled herself. Looked at him through the open door with one eyebrow high.

"Now, that suit hanging in your closet is another matter."

Heath quickly shut the car door and cast about for a subject change on his way to the driver's side.

———

ALL THINGS CONSIDERED, GRIPPER WASN'T ALL THAT FAR FROM HEATH'S apartment. Yes, it was across the river into the east side of Portland. In terms of cities, though, Portland wasn't all that big. And Gripper wasn't very far into the east side.

The way traffic just sort of moved aside for Heath's car, without a single driver realizing they were doing it — not to mention the way the stoplights seemed to go out of their way to usher his car through — total time from Heath's place to curb parking near Gripper couldn't have been eight minutes.

Even so, those were some of the longest minutes of Heath's year.

Nana Cyr firmly believed that every grown man should own a suit. She'd even emphasized the point to Heath before he'd moved to Portland.

He was to get himself a suit.

Even if he only wore it to weddings and funerals. Even if — as he told her on the phone — Portland wasn't the kind of city where people wore suits all that often.

No, he was to buy himself a suit. She'd made that quite clear. And so, not long after Heath found a place to live, he had gone out and bought himself a *suit*.

Of course, the store he went to was of the thrift variety, and at the time he was more concerned about his total investment than he was about the look of a suit he never intended to wear.

In all fairness, Heath didn't have much money or any kind of client base when he first moved to Portland.

So, the suit he'd bought was a faded burgundy color. And it was so big that Heath, Nariko *and* Colin could probably all have worn it at the same time. He'd bought himself a white, long-sleeved suit shirt to go with it, of course.

Well, once upon a time, that shirt had been white. Much the same way the *Parakeet* had once been red.

And the tie, well, the tie was a dark paisley pattern that didn't look good under *any* light, but Heath particularly never wanted to see it under a *black* light. He just wasn't all that sure about the tie's history, when he'd chosen it. Only the price tag.

He'd bought the suit so he could honestly tell his grandmother he'd bought a suit.

He'd never planned on her *seeing* it.

Then again, he'd never planned on leaving her alone in his apartment, either. Probably should have packed the beast up and left it at the dry cleaners. Sure, it might not have survived a proper cleaning. The shirt likely held together by habit, and for all Heath knew, that tie, if cleaned, would turn out to be monochromatic.

Still, at least if he'd taken the thing to the cleaners, then when she asked — because she would definitely have asked — he could have honestly told her where it was without giving her a chance to inspect it.

Yeah. That might have worked.

Maybe if he hadn't had so many things on his mind...

Instead, by the time Heath rolled his car to a stop behind Nariko's beautiful silver BMW motorcycle on a little side street east of the Willamette, Nana Cyr had made quite clear her unfettered disdain for that miserable excuse for a suit. Not to mention just how disappointed in him she was that he'd clearly tried to treat a good, grand-motherly request made out of love and concern as an opportunity to try to trick her. As though he *could.*

Finally, she laid down the law. She was not leaving Portland until Heath had bought himself a proper, *tailored* suit, made by people who knew what they were doing.

Worse, Heath had the feeling that Nariko would take great joy in coming along for the fitting to play dress-up with Heath. Throw in her own opinions about fabrics and colors for the suit itself, not to mention shirts and ties.

And shoes. Apparently Heath needed proper shoes and a belt to go with the rest.

Well, at least he could afford it now.

Of course, Heath suspected that once he *owned* such a suit, Nariko would find excuses for him to *wear* it.

On the other hand...

If Heath wore a suit that nice for Nariko, no doubt she would be wearing a dress that went *with* the suit...

All right, maybe it wouldn't be so bad after all.

In any event, they had arrived.

Heath was only too glad to get back out of his car and into the cooling air of the September evening. The sky purpled up above, and stars were just starting to show their faces. Not too many clouds yet, but a couple of spotlights cut across the night sky, trying to draw attention to some evening activity or other.

Gripper's side street was pretty typical for the slower parts of Portland's east side. Not more than a block off of a major street like Burnside, but it might as well have been a ghost town, for all the traffic it saw.

Of course, part of that was that most of the storefronts along the block were closed. Like the salvage shop on one side of Gripper, and the music shop on the other.

Nana Cyr hummed a sound of disapproval as she looked over the building they crossed the street to approach. Heath could understand why. Didn't look like a bar. Didn't even look like the kind of place anyone would *want* to approach.

Its shade of brown stucco was closer to something coming out the wrong end of a dog than something most people would consider "inviting." No windows. No sign.

"Don't like drawing in custom, do they?" she said as though pronouncing doom.

"I know you don't need me to tell you about the spells laid on this place," Heath said.

"Of course not," Nana Cyr replied. "But they might be the spells protecting any kind of bus—" She frowned. Looked up and down the block.

"Subtle," she said. "Owner picked a block with no other spellwork of any kind, and not only set up some good defensive measures, but left just a little tickle of invitation, for anyone who decided to look."

"Yep," Heath said, smiling. "Gripper is a place only for those who practice. Wannabes can cross the river and do their drinking at Croatoan."

"Odd name."

"Some kind of witch thing, I think. Plays well with the wannabes."

"What's Gripper mean?" she asked as they reached the door.

The door of Gripper was the only thing about the bar that might look inviting to the naked eye. It was bright red, with a purple number four done in a fancy style.

Well, it looked like the number four. According to Maggie, the owner, it was the symbol of Jupiter, a god of business.

"It's a nickname for some old magician. The kind that wrote those dusty old grimoires."

Nana Cyr chuckled. "That'd be like you or me naming a place after, oh, I don't know, Marie Laveau and calling it Mare's."

Heath chuckled. He knocked, four beats because it was Friday, and that was the expected number.

More of Maggie's planetary magic stuff.

The door opened. Immediately the smell of Maggie's famous garlic fries wafted out, carried by the same air that carried strains of

Irish folk music, and drew a rumble from Heath's stomach, despite his fullness from his wonderful dinner.

Watching the door tonight — Mrs. Halloran.

Of course. Why was it that, whenever anything big and dangerous was going on in Heath's life, the bouncer for the evening was the one who liked him least? Or maybe *dis*liked him most. Tough call which was the proper way to think of it, really.

Mrs. Halloran, to the untrained observer, probably looked like an innocuous old woman. On the frail side of seventy, with skin so white her wrinkles were almost translucent. Her silver hair fell to her shoulders as though somehow this were its natural state and never needed so much as a brush.

The sort of person who belonged at Gripper, though, could tell at a glance that Mrs. Halloran was a magical badass. Not someone that anyone would want to start trouble with, even if she *weren't* wearing that silver Celtic knotwork torc where she housed her dangerous familiar.

She was wearing the torc, though. Then again, Heath had never seen her without it.

To go with the torc tonight, she wore a simple gown of emerald green, matching her eyes, and she made the look regal. Or maybe that was the disdain with which she looked down on the world. Or at least down on Heath.

"Well, well," Mrs. Halloran said in her Old World lilt, "if it isn't the twilight boy, come to see us again."

Accompanying her words came that powdery-sweet perfume she wore. Heath noted she'd only opened the door halfway, and blocked the entrance with her body.

Nana Cyr took in the sight of Mrs. Halloran and set her spine and jaw in a way Heath hadn't seen often.

He immediately worried that he was going to have to stop a fight. Half of that worry was wondering if he even could stop a fight between these two...

"This a public establishment, or isn't it?" Nana Cyr said, glaring straight into Mrs. Halloran's eyes.

"Sure, and it's a place of business, if that's what you're asking," Mrs. Halloran said, appearing to notice Heath's grandmother for the first time. "Privately owned it is, though, so—"

"You know damn well what I'm asking. Is this a bar? Does it rely on the public for its custom?"

"Well..." Was Mrs. Halloran actually taken aback? "That it tis. But we don't allow in just—"

"Don't allow in what? Black people?" Nana Cyr looked Mrs. Halloran up and down again, not looking the least bit impressed by what she saw, before staring straight into the woman's eyes once more. "Or are you the type to call us colored? Or maybe prefer something starting with an 'n'?"

Heath's breath caught. His heart started pounding double time and his hands came up to intervene.

Both women ignored him.

"We here at Gripper cater to practitioners of the occult arts, whatever their heritage or nationality."

"Well then," Nana Cyr said. "Are you going to stand aside and let us in? Or are you so inept you can't tell we qualify?"

Mrs. Halloran's eyes darkened three shades. Power crawled along her skin. Heath could feel that familiar of hers stirring in its torc.

But Nana Cyr didn't offer anything but that deadly glare of hers.

"Well, and you must be the twilight boy's kin—"

"His name, to you, is *Mr. Cyr*, until he tells you otherwise."

"I know his name." Mrs. Halloran smiled now, slow and shallow. "I also know he has a history of causing trouble—"

"Here?" Nana Cyr pointed at the mostly closed red door. "Are you saying my grandson has *caused* trouble here? Started fights? Committed crimes?"

Heath knew that tone. His grandmother didn't believe any of that in the least.

"Seems to me he draws the attention of a bad element—"

"Then it seems to *me*," Nana Cyr said, stepping right up nose-to-nose with Mrs. Halloran, "that you ought to do more about keeping 'bad elements' out of this bar, and stop hassling those who don't *actually* cause trouble."

"Well, I—"

"*Mórai!*" Maggie's voice, likely calling from behind the bar. That was the name she used for her grandmother.

Mrs. Halloran stopped whatever she'd started to say. Glanced back over her shoulder, where Heath could just make out Maggie saying something in ... Irish? He didn't realize Maggie spoke Irish.

Mrs. Halloran shook her head, but turned back to face Heath and his grandmother with her lips drawn into a tight line and her narrow, bitchy nostrils flaring in a sigh that didn't seem to expand her skinny ribcage an inch.

She gave them an insincere smile, then held out one hand, palm up.

"Rules of the house," Heath quickly assured his grandmother as he took off his backpack. "No one gets to come into Gripper as heavily armed as I am when I have this thing."

"Hope you don't plan on taking my purse," Nana Cyr said.

"Not nearly so much in there as in that knapsack of his, now is there?" Mrs. Halloran said, not looking away from Heath.

He handed over the backpack. Mrs. Halloran stepped aside and gestured for them to enter.

AIR CONDITIONING MUST HAVE BEEN RUNNING AT GRIPPER MOST OF THE day, for it to be this cool when Heath and his grandmother entered.

The bar was decorated in Maggie's personal tribute to planetary magic.

The ceiling was painted black as outer space, but with a few swirls of blue and red to represent nebulae. Scattered across it were tiny lights, that both represented stars and guaranteed at least dim illumination in a bar that never got all that bright.

The floor was some kind of hardwood, but it was painted like the ceiling. Only the stars were painted in place, not actual lights.

The tables came in two varieties. Lots of little tables along the walls and across the floor, every one of them a dark shade of brown.

There were round tables too, of varying sizes, but only seven. And they were colorful: black, blue, red, yellow, green, orange and silver. Surrounded by the small brown tables, the colorful ones always reminded Heath of marshmallows in a bowl of breakfast cereal.

Now, those colorful tables had something to do with the planets, but Heath had never gotten a good answer about why there were only seven. In his mind, there should have either been eight or nine, depending on one's opinion of Pluto.

Maggie, however, felt differently. And it was her bar.

Speaking of the bar, it was a little worn and scuffed, but it was covered — top and sides — with hundreds of star charts, all safely protected by many layers of lacquer.

No mirror behind the bar. Not at a place like Gripper, where the right kind of drunk might have summoned the wrong kind of thing using a great big mirror...

Instead, the wall behind the bar was dedicated to alcohol. Shelves and shelves of it, from the cheapskate bourbons and vodkas to the top shelf obscure Irish whiskeys so old they might have predated the country they were being sold in.

The crowd was light so far, but it was early.

Along one wall, eight old men and women had pushed together four small brown tables, rather than take one of the bigger ones. The group had a distinctly Eastern European look, but Heath couldn't get more specific about them than that. And hell, the beards the men had fit right in among much of Portland's populace.

That was the largest single group though. Scattered throughout the bar, twos and threes, were a broad mixture of others. Mostly people Heath recognized, and some he'd say he even knew a bit. A couple of the *curanderos* — Jose and Maria — were laughing about something.

Hár, a tall, one-eyed Viking type with honey blonde hair and beard, big on rune magic, was sitting talking to DeAndre McDaniels.

DeAndre was one of the few other rootworkers in town who practiced Hoodoo. Though Heath always thought the man looked more like his street gangster roots.

Little shorter than Heath, DeAndre, but he made up the difference in mass and, Heath had to admit, style. His suit was a shade of blue that Nariko would call "cerulean," and it really set off his three gold rings. Not to mention the diamond tie tack in his matching tie. His dark-skinned bald head was polished a fine sheen tonight.

DeAndre, talking to Hár. Huh. Heath had always gotten along well with Hár, whereas DeAndre had always been ... rather aggressively a rival. At least, until quite recently.

Maybe DeAndre was trying to mend some fences with Hár too? Interesting.

Maggie was behind the bar, looking just about as pissed as Heath had ever seen her. And on Maggie, pissed looked dangerous. Not just because she was a pretty fair hand with her planetary magic, either. Not even because she had a nose that had been broken and reset *at least* once.

No, Maggie was lean with muscle, and *taught* mixed martial arts three days a week. She kept her red hair buzzed short, and tonight wore a tee shirt that had the collar and sleeves ripped off, as well as enough of the bottom to show off her six-pack abs. Didn't have to see the rest of Maggie to know she was wearing sturdy blue jeans. She always did.

Fortunately, that pissed off expression wasn't aimed at Heath. Nor at Heath's grandmother, but at her own, perched where Mrs. Halloran was on her bar stool over near the front door.

She'd put Heath's bag away someplace safe, but Heath never knew exactly where that was.

"I am *so* sorry about that," Maggie said, before Heath could even pull a stool out for his grandmother, much less sit on his own.

Nana Cyr made a noncommittal noise as she gave Maggie an assessing look that didn't indicate she cared for what she saw.

"No," Maggie said, speaking mainly to Nana Cyr, and only just remembering to glance at Heath as she spoke. "My grandmother usually enjoys giving Heath a hard time, but that. That was *way* over the line."

"That's one way to say it," Nana Cyr said, and from the way she was looking over Maggie, she seemed to be reconsidering her assessment, but the jury wasn't done yet. "Bet she gave that gentleman just as hard a time though, didn't she?"

Nana Cyr indicated DeAndre with a nod of her head.

"I..." Maggie sighed quickly through her nose. "I was in the back. Can't be sure. But I can't say she hasn't given him a hard time in the past. Still, she's always been harder on Heath."

"Seems to me," Nana Cyr said, her voice neutral, "that your grandmother is the kind of woman who was happier when there were *two sets* of drinking fountains."

"I—" Maggie started, but Nana Cyr wasn't done.

"Might also be that she isn't as worried about your taking a fancy to a man as heavy as that one, whereas my grandson here—"

"Is *way* out of my league," Maggie said, then raised her hands in surrender. "I really am sorry. And I will speak to her about it later. She's a powerful witch, but if she can't treat my customers with respect — especially my *favorite* customers — then she'll have to find another retirement job."

"Favorite?" That got a smile out of Nana Cyr. "Young lady, I believe this might be a place I wish to drink after all."

Maggie wasn't quite ready to stop apologizing.

"Please do," she said, "and rest assured that both your tabs are on my grandmother tonight. Straight out of her next paycheck."

Nana Cyr nodded in approval and looked over the selection while Maggie grabbed a plate of garlic fries for them both, and a glass of Deschutes Hefeweizen for Heath without bothering to wait for him to ask.

"If you want anything special," Maggie said, while Nana Cyr was still deciding, "let me know. I have a few items that, shall we say, aren't on the official menu."

Nana Cyr settled for a fine, if very expensive, glass of bourbon. But when Maggie presented it — with a longer pour than usual, if

Heath was not mistaken, Nana Cyr reached out and took Maggie's free wrist.

"Now you listen to me for a moment."

Maggie gave Nana Cyr her whole attention. Heath, by reflex, kept half of his own on the conversations around him, in case anyone said something that would draw his attention.

"My grandson is off the market, it's true. Quite possibly for good. Anyone who's ever seen him with his Nariko *must* know that."

Maggie smiled the kind of smile that seemed to lift the spirits of the whole room. But Nana Cyr wasn't done talking.

"But do not *ever* say again that *anyone* is 'out of your league.' You are a *very* pretty girl, with a dazzling smile. Not to mention that those clear blue eyes of yours likely bewitch half the men who see them, whether you realize it or not. 'Specially good as you are with that subtle eye makeup."

"But—"

"Some men might be put off by your muscles, it's true. But forget them. Those men would never suit you anyway. So you trust me. There is *no man* who is 'out of your league.'" Nana Cyr cocked her head to one side.

"Mrs. Cyr," Maggie started, then frowned. "It is Cyr, isn't it?"

"It is," Nana Cyr said proudly.

"Mrs. Cyr, your drinks are on the house anytime you want to drink here. Even on nights my grandmother doesn't insult you." She turned to Heath. "I *do* like her."

"Me too," Heath said with a smile. "Have to ask though. Seen Celia Martinez, Tommy Wong, or Stetson Price in here tonight?"

"Not in a couple of days," Maggie said, frowning not so much with her lips but with a crease between her shaped eyebrows. "Since when do you hang out with them?"

"I don't."

"They may have tried to kill him today," Nana Cyr said, and followed her words with a sip of bourbon.

Maggie's jaw dropped in shock.

"Don't know that for sure," Heath said quickly, while his grandmother said something about how smooth the bourbon was. "But they *are* on the short list of suspects."

"Only thing I've heard," Maggie said, "is that they're trying to organize something. Don't know what though."

Heath considered telling Maggie. After all, anyone wanting to form a council here in Portland would want Maggie on that council. She was already de facto in charge of the main public gathering place for the community.

But as he glanced around the room again, something more immediately pressing occurred to him.

"Seen Nariko?" Heath asked. "Her bike's outside, but—"

The front door of Gripper slammed open.

Now, Heath had done his drinking at Gripper a good many nights. Sometimes just to chat with Maggie, other times either talking shop or socializing with his peers. Sometimes even to prove a point, one way or another.

But in all the times he'd been to Gripper, that front door had only ever opened one way —by the hand of a bouncer, in response to the right number of knocks.

Until now.

The door slammed open, right in front of Mrs. Halloran's surprised face.

All conversations in the room stopped cold. Even the Irish music floating in over the hidden speakers stopped, though maybe that was just the end of the song. Folk music in general wasn't really Heath's thing.

Framed in the open door and backlit by sodium lamps in the growing night stood Nariko.

And she looked like fury personified.

She'd been spattered with blood, head to toe. Her hair was wild, and floating around her head like wind caught it. Her steel spike was in one fist, and her other hand was held up to ward off Mrs. Halloran.

"Heath," she said. "We need to move."

Heath's feet were moving before he even thought to ask his grandmother to stay here. But Nana Cyr was right beside him, and from the look on her face, she did *not* intend to sit by and do nothing.

"Maggie," Heath called over his shoulder as he hustled toward the door, "text Colin for me?"

"On it," Maggie said.

But suddenly between Heath and the doorway stood DeAndre McDaniels.

Heath hadn't known the big man could move that fast.

"Not now, DeAndre," Heath said, trying to go around.

"Let me help," he said in that deep voice of his.

That was unexpected enough to make Heath stop, if only long enough to give DeAndre a look of utter disbelief.

DeAndre took advantage of that pause to talk quickly.

"I mean it. No charge, either. After the way you and Brother Tony saved me... Let me do this. Let me prove I'm trying to turn things around."

No doubt this was turning into the strangest day Heath had had in quite a while.

"Nana Cyr," Heath said quickly, "this is DeAndre McDaniels, a man whose been my enemy more than he hasn't, but says he wants to change that. DeAndre, this is my grandmother, Mrs. Cyr."

"Pleasure," DeAndre said, giving Nana Cyr a smile that showed a lot of big, bright teeth.

"Hope I'll be able to say the same, Mr. McDaniels."

"Let's move," Heath said.

If DeAndre really were ready and willing to help, he could be a real boon right now. Heath couldn't help thinking, though, that if DeAndre were trying to trick him, he'd kill the big man and not lose even a minute's sleep over doing it.

"I told you," Mrs. Halloran said from her perch as the three of them reached the door. "The twilight boy is trouble."

But she tossed Heath his backpack, so Heath let her have her precious last word.

The moment Heath reached Nariko she turned and started walking at a brisk clip, talking as she went.

"There was a team of three hitters waiting for you. They'd set up in two spots, ready to catch you in a crossfire, and this time they had magic supporting them. They were ready for your counter-charms."

"Get any information out of them?" Heath asked, glancing to check on Nana Cyr, but the tough old woman was keeping pace well. And DeAndre had fallen back to take up the rear, watching all directions like he knew what he was doing.

Probably did. Given what he used to do.

"Had to kill the shooters," Nariko said. "The other took a suicide pill before I could stop him."

"Dedicated group," Heath said. "What's the hurry then?"

"The two-man side had an overseer. I've still got a feel for it."

An overseer. A watcher spirit intended to report on results.

"Keep moving," DeAndre called. "I'll grab my ride and catch up."

"Sure about him?" Nariko asked.

Heath gave her a droll look. "Need to give him a chance though."

"Tony's a bad influence on you."

"Only sinners need a second chance," Nana Cyr said. "And this one feels sincere to me."

Highest praise anyone could have given DeAndre McDaniels, far as Heath was concerned.

Speaking of DeAndre, he was pulling up beside them right now in his huge, shiny black Lexus LX450. Nearest window buzzed down.

"Get in," he said.

Nana Cyr got the front seat. Nariko sat behind DeAndre, and Heath behind his grandmother.

"Straight three blocks," Nariko said, "then right."

DeAndre drove like he wasn't worried about accidents or tickets. Heath didn't even need to check to know that meant he had all his charms working again.

"Why don't *you* drive a car like this, Heath?" Nana Cyr asked over her shoulder, while Nariko muttered more directions to DeAndre.

"Something big and comfortable. Something a grandmother could feel proud to be seen in."

The answer that he loved his little Gremlin wasn't going to cut it.

"For one thing, I don't want anyone seeing me behind the wheel," he said. "Besides. Be wasted on me anyway. I like the feel I get for the city on public transit."

"Says the man who's been riding in Tony's and Colin's cars quite a bit lately," Nariko said, before returning to what she was telling DeAndre.

Text came in from Colin. "O.C. not involved. Coming to you."

O.C. Organized crime? Looked as though Heath was right about Tony's background.

"Any idea of our destination?" Heath asked, hoping to have something more to send back than *More shooters. Tracking a spirit.*

"Not sure," Nariko said, her voice a little distant as she focused on the overseer. "Where's Flex?"

"South of here," Heath said, glancing at the street signs. "Maybe a mile and a half. Little ways back toward the river."

"What's Flex got to do with this?" DeAndre asked.

"Someone hired them to take me out," Heath said. "Know anything about them?"

"Everything," he said. "I helped them set up in this town, before they got enough of a foothold to bring their own people in to handle their magic."

"Leave yourself any back doors?"

"I *am* a conjure man," he said, sounding affronted, but shooting Heath a big smile in the rearview mirror.

Heath couldn't help smiling right back.

Nana Cyr didn't react to that, but now that Heath paid attention, he could hear her muttering prayers, with power coming off of her that felt almost soft and fuzzy.

Whatever she was doing, he hoped it worked. And speaking of prayers…

"Papa Legba," Heath muttered, "look after this little fool and his friends. I need to live at least long enough to save Nariko from her mother."

"Mount Tabor Park!" Nariko said. "I can feel it now. The overseer is headed for Mount Tabor Park."

She was smiling now, a smile made all the more vicious by the blood still spattering her face.

Heath would have offered her a wet nap, but he knew she wouldn't take it. Not while on the hunt.

He took the moment instead to send Tony and Colin an update.

"Idiots," Nariko said. "Like I said before. Mount Tabor stands with *me*."

She had a point. The spirit of Mount Tabor was a pretty big deal, over here on the east side. And if Nariko could call it an ally, then she was walking into a place where she'd be even more powerful than usual.

Still, though, Heath couldn't shake the feeling that this was a trap.

6

Mount Tabor wasn't a mountain, per se. It was an extinct volcano. Had been extinct for a long, long time. Nariko probably knew how long. Maybe even down to the exact year. Heath just knew it died out a long, long time ago.

Nevertheless, the spirit of the volcano was alive and well. That seemed a little odd to Heath, but he was sure that it made sense to Nariko and her Shugendō.

Maybe when the volcano went extinct, its spirit merely shifted to accommodate?

Question for another time.

Not even as tall as some of the hills on the west side, Mount Tabor. Little more than six hundred feet or so. But it did spike up a bit over its surroundings, and somewhere along the way Portland had designated the area around it a park. Had an amphitheater, a little lake, even a basketball court around here somewhere.

Mostly, though, trails. Trails for hikers, trails for bikers, and trails for dogs. This was Portland, after all. Hiking, biking and dogs were evidently crucial to the Portland experience.

Almost made Heath wonder sometimes how he managed to avoid

getting a dog. 'Course, he did have a cat, so maybe that split the difference.

Plus, he hated bicyclists. Maybe there was some connection between bikes and dogs. Sounded like something Maggie would know. Or maybe Tony.

Of course, Colin would probably have a very amusing theory about it...

DeAndre found a parking spot along one of the roads that meandered through the park. Through the kind of coincidence that magic was fond of, it happened that the only other car parked in the area was the white Saturn sedan that Heath recognized as Colin's.

The evening air had picked up a bit of a chill. Sky was strangely clear overhead. Heath would have expected more cloud cover from a September evening, but the sky above showed Heath plenty of stars despite the street lights around him.

This park wasn't so wild as Forest Park. Even from where he stood, Heath thought the park smelled tamer. More grass and Douglas firs than anything else. Not the sheer variety of plants he'd have smelled at the park he favored.

Or maybe he was just worried he'd smell a trap.

Tony looked more like himself than a gangster in disguise as he and Colin approached. Even looked pleased to see DeAndre with the group, as opposed to Colin's wordless surprise.

Heath caught Tony and Colin up quickly. Tony nodded, and said, "I checked a couple of old sources. Doesn't seem like the hire came from anyone involved in criminal activities. We were on our way to Flex when we heard from Maggie."

"The overseer came here," Nariko said, and Colin's eyes tried to bug out of his head as he did a double-take at the sight of a very bloody Nariko. "This way."

She turned and started walking without another word.

"Might want a plan," Heath said.

"Have one," she said, and Heath and the others hurried to catch up with her as she continued. "Find the overseer. Either find the person its reporting to *right now* or capture the overseer and force it to help us."

"Vicious when there's trouble, isn't she?" Nana Cyr asked quietly. Too quietly for anyone but him to hear.

But before Heath could respond, Nariko said, "Someone is trying to kill Heath. They'll get no mercy from me."

Nana Cyr raised her eyebrows at Heath, not over Nariko's words — well, maybe *partially* over Nariko's words — but likely over the growing aura of power that surrounded Nariko as this allied location began to bolster her.

Her steps gained a bounce. Her hair was floating again.

And clearly her hearing had improved.

DeAndre fell in on Heath's other side. Tony and Colin brought up the rear.

"You know this is probably a trap, right?" DeAndre asked, even quieter than Nana Cyr'd been.

"Best way out of an ambush is through," Nariko said.

And there was nothing much to do then but follow her.

Nariko left the street, following a hiking path to the left. The route took them higher, but the slope wasn't too steep, so Heath wasn't too worried about his grandmother keeping up. Not yet.

He knew she could handle damn near anything magical that anyone tried to throw at her. But he wasn't sure about too quick a pace on a hill. She wasn't as young as she used to be.

"Nari," Heath said, hustling up to stride beside her, "we need to think about this."

"Done thinking. Done talking. I finally have a target, and I intend to do some damage. Send a message. Loud. And. Clear."

The path wound around a bit on its way up. But not long enough. Nariko might have been done thinking, but Heath wouldn't have minded a little more time to plan. Maybe send an observer or two of his own. Get a feel for what the crickets and frogs had to...

"Wait," Heath said, but Nariko didn't.

"Nari," he said, "it's too quiet."

And it was true. The birds weren't singing, not even the night birds. And surely this place had some frogs and crickets around that should have been offering up their opinions on public events. But if it did, they were keeping their own counsel right now.

Heath didn't like that at all.

Weren't any other *people* around either. Even though this park didn't officially close until midnight. Which meant there should have been *somebody* else around.

The evening joggers and hikers, maybe. Someone who'd been working all day, maybe, and only now got the chance to play with his dog.

Hell, even just a couple of stoners, toking up under the evening sky, or a couple of lovers making out.

Something.

But there was *nobody* else around.

And that, that just was not normal.

"Nari," Heath said, voice low and urgent, "I'm telling you it's too quiet."

"Good," she said. "No innocents to get caught in crossfire."

Heath glanced back at the others. Here on the hiking path there weren't so many lights, and he could see them only in the growing gray of the evening.

But from the faces he saw, he could tell that they, at least, understood his point and found it significant.

Nariko, unfortunately, was just *not* going to listen right now.

HEATH WAS STILL TRYING TO FIGURE OUT HOW TO GET NARIKO TO STOP and listen as they came around a curve to the left, heading more directly up the hillside.

She stopped, all on her own.

She wasn't looking at Heath though.

She was looking out over the grassy, sloping field to their left. Grass was a bit wild, like it was due for the mower. And despite the clear sky above, the air had picked up a hint like it might rain later tonight. Blended with the grassy smell.

Up around the top of the field, another path was crossing left to right. Douglas fir trees almost a loose ellipse around all four sides.

There was a flat, concrete circle up near the top of the slope, though. And just above that, built into the hillside, something that looked like a dark, ugly bunker. Rectangular warts coming off the sides for some kind of electronics.

He could feel the presence of the overseer now, floating in the air above the circle of concrete.

Two people stood on that circle, just below the overseer. Heath couldn't see them all that well, dim as the light was, but they were both thin, and Heath was pretty sure they were both...

Both women. One a little taller.

Heath had a sinking feeling in his stomach that he knew exactly who those two women were. And that was very, very bad.

Heath held his breath and opened his spirit eyes.

Yeah, the overseer was about what he expected. Little artificial thing, like a ball with a bunch of eyes and ears.

And the people were just who he thought they were: Mrs. Tachibana and Nariko's sister Kaida.

Used to be that, when Heath saw Mrs. Tachibana through his spirit eyes, she just looked like a more powerful version of Nariko. Physically, she might have stood maybe an inch or two taller, not to mention skinnier and showing the signs of age one might expect. But magically, she looked tough. But human.

Now, though, she wasn't hiding what she was any longer.

Heath saw the dragon, not the woman.

Scales like bronze and copper. Four powerful legs that were somehow enough for that long, long, *long* body.

Seriously, the dragon that was Mrs. Tachibana seemed to stretch out the rest of the way up Mount Tabor.

Her head looked big enough to swallow that bunker, and still have room for the concrete circle she stood on. Not to mention the six poor humans facing her.

She had drooping mustaches, too. Huh.

Kaida was an obvious contrast beside her.

Kaida was clearly a mountain dragon like her mother. Tiny, by comparison. No more than maybe a dozen feet long, not including the tail, so her legs seemed more ... proportionate to her body. Her scales were a bright copper color, with little hints of reds here and there.

And she had mustaches too. Must've been a dragon thing.

Kaida did feel powerful. Powerful enough to be a serious threat all on her own. But she paled beside the ancient power of Mrs. Tachibana.

Power that felt older and stronger than anything Heath had ever been near. Enough power that there might not even *be* a way to fight her, much less win.

Kaida started giggling. Disconcerting, hearing a dragon giggle. But she was and wasn't a dragon right now, same as her mother. Both of those women were still women, physically. Their dragon nature showed only in their spirits right now.

But Heath had the awful feeling that that was going to change very soon...

There was only one good thing that Heath could see right now. Well, beyond the impressive aura of power Nariko had going.

Heath could see the spirit of Mount Tabor as well. Old. Maybe as old as Mrs. Tachibana, maybe not. But it was big. Powerful too.

But was it powerful enough to make the difference?

"Trying to have my boyfriend killed?" Nariko challenged. "That's low even for you, Mother."

"Only a distraction," Mrs. Tachibana said. "Though I wouldn't have minded if they succeeded."

"I fooled you!" Kaida taunted in a sing-song voice. "I fooled you and you had no idea."

"Sounds like she's twelve," DeAndre said, disapproving.

"Too spoiled to really grow up, emotionally," Colin said.

Nana Cyr hushed them, then said softly, "Nariko, tell your big ally here to work with me."

Nariko didn't look away from her mother and sister, but she nodded. And while she did whatever she did next, Heath stepped forward.

"Please," Heath said. "Little thing like you couldn't pull the wool over my eyes if I was tied to a chair and wearing a woolen balaclava."

"Shut up!" Kaida said, voice rougher now.

"We both know your mother here sent you out with bad information. Didn't trust you to handle anything important."

Mrs. Tachibana casually waved one hand in the air, and Heath felt the spirits of two of his protective conjure hands just … shatter.

Caught his breath and staggered him back a step.

"Heath Cyr," she said, and her voice was lower and rougher too, now, "you have been an irritant for far too long. I think, perhaps, I'll eat you first."

Power shifted up the hill. The spirit form of the mountain dragon that Heath knew as Mrs. Tachibana seemed to surge forward, in place.

There was a feeling to the air. Like a balloon getting squeezed tighter and tighter, but not yet popping.

The pop was coming. It had to be. No balloon could get squeezed that tight and not pop.

Then Heath smelled the clean scent of Florida water. And he realized he could hear prayer. Soft prayers coming from his grandmother, counterpoint to the rattle of her shaking *asson*.

The *asson* just looked like a gourd with a natural handle, covered in a netting of colorful beads. But it was the scepter of power for a *manbo*.

The language she prayed in was French. And the Lwa she called were Damballah Wedo and Aida Wedo. The husband and wife serpents. Sometimes together referred to as the serpent and the rainbow.

One the earth. The other the sky.

That pressure in the air seemed to balance itself. Tight, but not popping.

Kaida snapped out something in Japanese, but her mother silenced her with a wave of her hand.

Nariko started laughing, and Heath joined her. No one else did. They must not have understood yet. Well, Nana Cyr knew, but she was busy.

"Can't shift, can you?" Nariko taunted, her voice husky with power. "Both stuck in your human forms. Looks like this may be a fair fight after all."

SHOULD'VE BEEN A FULL MOON.

Here it was a deserted park, tucked away on an extinct volcano in eastern Portland. Two mountain dragons — stuck in their human forms for as long as Nana Cyr could keep them that way — both spoiling for a fight.

Heath and Nariko facing them, backed by Tony, Colin and DeAndre.

Gentle breeze wafting the thick grass. The air tense with power.

Really should have had a full moon overhead to complete the scene.

But while Heath's life had more than enough real drama to suit any ten people (well, maybe not any ten *teenagers*), it was sadly lacking in the kind of cinematic drama that might have made this moment cool.

So instead, it was only about a half-moon up above. Good selection of stars at least, but the stars didn't shine bright enough to make the surroundings more than shades of gray. And the nearest lights on the hiking paths weren't much help.

"Wait!" Tony cried out, hustling forward with both hands raised. "Wait!"

All eyes turned to Tony.

"You are *family*," Tony implored. "Blood. Mother and children. Surely this need not come to violence."

"Who is this?" Mrs. Tachibana asked, turning her eyes back to Nariko.

It was Tony who answered.

"My name is Brother Antonio, and I just want to help. Whatever problems there may be between you, surely they need not descend into violence. Enough blood has been shed tonight."

Mrs. Tachibana cocked her head to the side, still looking at Nariko. "Whose blood *is* that on your face and clothes, by the way?"

"Your assassins'. Disappointed?"

"Certainly not. You're my daughter. If you could not kill three assassins without injury to yourself, you would not be worth feeding to your sister."

"Eww," Colin said. "That has to be the grossest thing I've—"

"Enough prattle," Mrs. Tachibana said. "Kaida, tend to your sister while I—"

"No!" Nariko said, with enough power coursing through her to make her voice echo like thunder.

"Mother," she said, taking her steel hair spike in one hand and shaking out her long locks, "you intended to kill me from at least the birth of Kaida. You have tried to control me my whole life. If you want me dead, come kill me yourself."

Mrs. Tachibana actually made an impatient sound.

"Don't speak foolishness," and she rattled off Japanese so fast she might have been reciting an epic poem in the space of five seconds.

Nariko shotgunned more Japanese right back at her.

Then Tony yelled something in Japanese, and everyone was looking at him again.

"I'll continue in Japanese, if that's the only way to get through to you," he said. "But this fight *must not happen*. The least you can do is discuss the problems between you and find another path."

"Tony," Heath said, fighting down a sigh. "Words aren't going to help here. That's not a woman, that's a monster. And the logic she follows has very little to do with human logic, or the value of human life or blood or spirit. Except, maybe, as it serves her needs."

"Just so," Nariko said. "So, Mother. You must know that here, in a place of strength, I am too much for Kaida. Especially if she cannot take her dragon shape. Let's settle this you and—"

"Kaida, kill her while I deal with her friends."

"Stop my sister!" Nariko yelled out.

Nariko leapt high into the air. Dozens of feet up. The kind of leap that Heath had never seen outside of a movie. And she came down right at her mother.

But her mother was ready for her and dodged out of the way.

Nariko dented the hillside beneath her with a boom that shook Heath where he stood.

"Get Kaida," Heath barked at Colin.

Colin smiled, but it wasn't a happy or vicious smile. It was more...

Heath didn't have the word for it. It was somehow supportive and willing, but not really happy about what he was doing.

It was a smile of pure Colin. That was the only way Heath could think of it.

But Colin started calling spirits out of everywhere with speed that even Heath found impressive. Artificial spirits, of a sort, that wouldn't have any existence at all, if he didn't call them.

True to Colin's ... less aggressive nature, these artificial spirits wouldn't do any actual damage. Instead they distracted and deceived. Baffled senses, trying to overwhelm their foe into submission.

None of Colin's spirits on their own would be enough to stop Kaida, much less her mother, but he was calling so many so fast they were going to at least help. Already Kaida was fighting *them* and not Colin.

But those spirits wouldn't be enough.

"You two, help him," Heath said, slinging off his backpack. "Leave the mother to Nariko and me."

Nariko and her mother were spouting Japanese at each other — and Mrs. Tachibana barked more at Kaida as well — while Nariko kept up a flurry of attacks that would probably have cut their way through a hundred ninjas.

Not enough for one ancient mountain dragon though, even one in human form. Mrs. Tachibana kept dodging and blocking. Not attacking yet, but probably only holding back to give her youngest a chance to intervene.

Scariest part about watching the dizzying speed of Mrs. Tachibana in holding off Nariko? Mrs. Tachibana was doing it all in some kind of traditional Japanese dress that by all rights should have been way too tight to fight in.

Heath trotted closer as he watched, but not too close. No reason to make himself a physical target.

Heath dug into his backpack. Pulled out the small portable incense censer he'd dubbed the bedpan, along with his engraved wooden box of incenses.

He quickly got a special combination going on top of a burning coal. Built on a base of dragon's blood and asafetida, along with a few other things, the combination of smells was pretty foul. But that would be true of anything involving asafetida.

This combination, though, was something Heath had put together that would be good against a Japanese mountain dragon. If it did its job right, it would seep into Mrs. Tachibana and Kaida, and weaken them from within.

It had taken Heath a few weeks of research and experimentation to figure out what he needed to make this incense, and in what proportions. But ever since Nariko had confessed what her mother was and what her mother seemed to have in mind, he'd started making preparations for this fight.

Nariko kept up the whirl of attacks. Punches, kicks, swirling and leaping. And yet, Heath knew the real fight was still to come. This was not going to be a simple martial arts exhibition. No, Nariko had more she could and should be doing...

Oh. Of course. She was keeping her mother's attention to get Heath in the game. Get every edge he could give her before she took her best shot. Because she might only get one.

He could almost have slapped himself in the forehead. Couldn't waste the time though. Instead he dug into his bag for one more crucial thing.

A few dozen feet away, Kaida screamed in frustration. And possibly pain.

From the corner of his eye, Heath could see that Colin was dancing around, staying out of reach as he continued to bring in his dazzling spirits at a rate that was almost staggering.

But that wasn't what had gotten to Kaida.

She'd come after Tony, possibly thinking he would be the easiest target to take out. But when she reached him, two things happened at once.

First, her fist never reached him. He was holding up his crucifix, and when her blow came, something flared white light and repelled her fist. As though Tony's aura had physical armor plating.

Tony might have been chanting in Latin, too. Too much talking to keep track of, among the French, Japanese and ... whatever.

What really got Kaida, though, had been DeAndre, who had a packet ready for her. When she'd swung at Tony, DeAndre blew a fistful of some kind of powder in her face, and she'd recoiled and jumped around like it burned her.

Neat blend, that. Heath would have to ask about it later.

Kaida's scream seemed to make Mrs. Tachibana take the fight more seriously.

She leapt over Nariko and landed *hard* on the grass next to her youngest daughter. Hard enough to shake the ground and send Tony, DeAndre and Colin tumbling. Heath, farther away from ground zero, had only shaken.

A quick glance said that Nana Cyr had stumbled but held her feet. And hadn't stopped her prayers for even a moment.

Mrs. Tachibana hefted DeAndre above her head with one hand, as though he'd weighed less than Heath. Maybe even less than a paperclip. But before she could throw the huge man, Nariko was there, landing a flying kick to the base of her spine.

The kick failed to level Mrs. Tachibana, but it did make her drop DeAndre, instead of throwing him. Might even have hurt her a little bit, though Heath couldn't be sure of that.

Down at the bottom of his bag, Heath's fingers finally found the crinkle of just the bit of aluminum foil he'd been looking for. Tucked right down against the lining, and held there with a piece of tape.

Heath pulled out that foil, while Nariko and her mother both exchanged blows and parries now, and the others tried to get after Kaida, who was still moaning and running in circles with more coordination than should have been fair under the circumstances.

His fingers out of the bag now, Heath unrolled the foil and pulled out his prize. A prize he'd never wanted to use. A prize he'd collected months ago, after Mrs. Tachibana — protesting the entire time — had helped Nariko save Heath's life.

Probably regretted it ever since. She'd regret it even more soon.

Saving Heath's life after that snapper attack had involved baths and incense and a different kind of magic than Heath used, all done in a bathroom of the Tachibana household.

A bathroom where Heath had found, on the floor beside the sink, one single long, black strand of hair with just a hint of gray toward one end. A strand that just a little magical investigation had proven came from Mrs. Tachibana herself.

She'd never liked Heath, and he'd known even then that she was powerful. So he'd taken that strand of hair as an insurance policy.

Never even told Nariko he'd done it.

But as he held up that strand of hair, he sure was glad he'd taken it.

Colin, Tony and DeAndre were doing a good job of keeping Kaida busy. Though, admittedly, DeAndre was still trying to get his wits back together after Mrs. Tachibana had dropped him.

Nariko and Mrs. Tachibana were still going at it, and now there was more magic to their fight. Every swing and counter wasn't just physical now, but a channeling of power. Nariko's steel hair spike glowed a pale blue in her right hand.

Speaking of channeling power, Heath was ready to make use of that strand of Mrs. Tachibana's hair.

He couldn't hurt Mrs. Tachibana with it. At least, not much. Not here and now. No, he'd need more than a little preparation before he could reach out and do serious harm to a creature as old and powerful as her. Even *with* a bit of her hair.

But he knew what he *could* do here and now, especially with that incense going, playing just a little havoc on any dragons in the immediate area.

He held that strand of hair in the smoke, and began praying his own spin on a Bible verse he deemed appropriate. "Grab that dragon and bind for her a thousand years!"

Sure, King James might not have approved of the phrasing, but Heath had always found a personal, meaningful spin on scripture more effective than any fancy language.

He held the strand in the smoke. Kept his attention on just what his goal was — binding the power of his enemy — and focused hard on his little twist of a verse from Revelations.

In the meantime, Kaida had gathered herself again, while DeAndre was starting to find his way toward his feet. Tony stood over him, protective, crucifix held high. Colin kept moving, and kept calling out more of his artificial spirits.

It was like he was a doorman, letting eager fans into a rock concert — one at a time, as fast as they could come. And all headed right at Kaida.

Mrs. Tachibana slowed for a moment. Maybe felt Heath's magic reaching for her, despite any powers or charms she might have had to keep him away.

That hesitation almost got her caught by one of Nariko's kicks.

Heath smiled and focused harder. His trick hadn't quite taken hold yet — even with the hair, she was still a damned old mountain dragon — so he held his focus tight to his will.

Mrs. Tachibana snapped to attention. Leaped backward through the air just ahead of Nariko's punch. Nariko sprang right after her.

Kaida spun and opened her mouth so wide, Heath expected her jaw to drop like a snake's.

Power came flooding out of her mouth. Likely what Nariko would have called "ki." A torrent of it straight at Colin, Tony and DeAndre...

Swing and a miss. Her power failed to get through Colin's personal defenses, whereas when it reached Tony, that white light flared again and the flood of power just died out right there.

Yeah, she'd taken down a number of Colin's spirits along the way, but he was still calling more.

A puff of grayish smoke left her mouth then. Actual, physical smoke, but not a lot of it.

Colin made a sad trombone noise.

Kaida grabbed the sides of her head, shaking. Maybe Colin's spirits were finally starting to get to her.

"Mom?" Kaida sounded unsure of herself for a moment. Every bit the teenager she was. Tony started talking to her, softly, in English. Likely trying to get her to stop fighting and surrender. Possibly even offering to find her help of some sort.

Just the kind of guy Tony was.

Mrs. Tachibana, though, must have figured out that her daughter's fire breathing — or whatever was supposed to physically accompany that blast of power — was on the fritz. Maybe thanks to the incense. Maybe a side effect of Nana Cyr's invocation of Damballah Wedo and Aida Wedo. Maybe just too much pressure from the fight, for a kid who'd been way too spoiled all her life.

Either way, Mrs. Tachibana decided to handle the matter herself. She spun, crouched with one leg out and both arms high and wide. She dropped her own jaw then. And her jaw dropped like it really had unhinged. Probably could have taken a good-sized watermelon into her mouth without touching her teeth.

Heath threw everything he had into that binding.

No fire came out of her either, with that breath. Not even smoke.

But the power. Oh, dear God, the *power*.

That blast of power slammed right into Tony, Colin and DeAndre. Burned right through Colin's wards, Tony's white-light-shield, not to mention whatever DeAndre had for protections. And it might have blasted them to nothing—

—except it cut off all of a sudden.

Heath's binding, finally taking hold.

Mrs. Tachibana's mouth was open like more power was supposed to be coming out, but no more power came.

What she'd fired off had more than done the job, though, far as Heath was concerned. Tony, Colin and DeAndre were all down, and rolling their way down the hillside. They were all groaning, so at least none of them were *dead*, but that was the only good Heath could see in it.

Small blessing at the moment, though. Because Mrs. Tachibana must have felt that binding and figured out the source.

She turned to Heath, and right then he couldn't afford worry about his friends.

She screamed in fury and leaped high into the air.

Heath looked up at Mrs. Tachibana, streaking through the air towards him. Tried desperately to think of an emergency measure that wouldn't steal enough focus to ruin his binding.

There was nothing. Holding that binding took everything he had.

To save himself, he'd have to give it up.

But if he gave up the binding, Nariko would lose. Get taken down by her mother. Consumed by her sister.

His Nariko. Nari. Dead and gone.

Never.

Mrs. Tachibana might kill him, but Heath would hold that binding through his last breath.

Hell, he'd hold that binding until Papa Ghede came to carry his angel back across the waters.

So this moment of looking up at the incoming flying kick of Mrs. Tachibana, this might be the last moment of his life.

The world seemed to slow down. Heath could see every thread of the smooth black fabric along the bottom of the slipper coming for his throat.

Heath figured the way he felt right then had to be the way a field mouse felt, looking up into the talons of a striking hawk.

He did the only thing he could think of. The only thing he could do without ruining his binding.

He flipped her off.

Mrs. Tachibana was still screaming in rage as she descended.

But Nariko somehow got there first.

She stood over Heath, stance wide and balanced. Hands behind her waist, then thrusting forward with a *kiai* so powerful that the sound alone cracked that huge nearby concrete circle in half.

In that movement, Nariko thrust a ki strike at her mother with everything she had.

Knocked her mother right out of the air.

Mrs. Tachibana was holding her chest when she hit the ground. All of Mount Tabor shook when she hit.

"Mom!" Kaida called out, running over, crying. Mrs. Tachibana moved one hand to hold her youngest daughter back, already to her knees on her way back to her feet.

"Your spell..." Mrs. Tachibana was panting for breath as she addressed Heath. "...will not ... hold me ... long."

She stood now. Listing a bit to the right, and still holding her ribs. But her eyes glowed golden, serpentine and dangerous.

"He can hold you long enough, Mother," Nariko said, crackling with yet more power. "Long enough for me to kill you. If you make me."

"No!" Tony's groaned objection was weak, but audible.

Mrs. Tachibana narrowed her eyes. "I sense more mountains within you. You have been busy."

"I do not want to kill you, Mother. Any more than I want to hurt Kaida."

Mrs. Tachibana began to smile an evil smile.

"But I *will* kill you both right now, if I must. Give me any reason and I will not hesitate. As things stand, you *cannot* prevail. And Kaida" — Nariko shook her head — "won't even be a fight."

Kaida was crying openly now, eyes red and tears streaming down her cheeks.

Mrs. Tachibana spat some Japanese at her youngest. Nariko said something else to her sister. Something softer.

"You were raised to be food for my next dragon child," Mrs. Tachibana said to Nariko. "What peace do you think you can have?"

"Swear to me that you and yours will leave us in peace for so long as we and our descendants shall live. Swear this for me, for Heath, his family, my *human* family, and my friends. Swear these things by our ancestors—"

"Our ancestors—"

"And by Amaterasu. Swear these things right now, and I will not kill you where you stand."

"You ask a great deal."

"You are immortal," Nariko said simply. "Unless someone kills you. Do you value your life *less* than what I ask?"

Mrs. Tachibana laughed. A pained laugh, true, but a laugh all the same.

"Very well, child."

The rest of what passed between them then was in Japanese, so Heath couldn't really assess the quality of the oath. But he trusted Nariko.

Mrs. Tachibana spoke English then, addressing Heath.

"Your spell. Remove it."

"It's safe," Nariko said with a nod.

Heath squeezed the fist that held that strand of hair. But he closed the lid on the bedpan, and he spat a bit of power to the ground, cutting off his jinx.

Mrs. Tachibana immediately rolled her shoulders. She gave Nariko a look Heath couldn't quite interpret, but then turned and leaped into the sky.

"Can I..." Kaida swallowed. "Can I call you?"

"Do it soon," Nariko said. "Mom's going to take tonight out on someone, and Michiko and Dad aren't options anymore."

Kaida nodded, but then leaped into the sky and away.

"They can fly?" Heath asked.

"They *are* dragons," Nariko said, and then the two of them turned and hustled down the slope to check on their friends.

———

THE NIGHT AIR FELT CLEANER AND COOLER NOW, WITH THE DRAGONS gone. Brighter too, as though Mrs. Tachibana had been doing something to the dim the light coming from the nearby hiking paths.

Not that it would have surprised Heath to learn that Mrs. Tachibana just made the world a darker place wherever she was.

Whatever fuel he'd gotten from that nap and dinner, he'd just about burned away. Wouldn't say he was quite dead on his feet, but this had been one hell of a day.

Getting home, fixing a snack, and curling up with Nariko sounded like the best of all possible courses of action.

First though, he had to see about everyone else.

Heath could see Nana Cyr moving around, still off to one side. On her feet, and doing something. Likely making offerings to Damballah Wedo and Aida Wedo, in thanks for their aid.

Sounded like a good idea. Heath would have to remember to make his own offerings of thanks later. He had no doubt that without the aid of the Lwa through his grandmother, this fight would have been short, ugly and fatal.

Colin, Tony and DeAndre were all sitting against Douglas fir trees, down at the bottom of the grassy slope. They all looked conscious, which was something.

Still, best to check on their physical states first.

Colin complained loudly that his whole body was one giant, sore bruise. He could move though, if gingerly, and didn't seem to have any long-term physical damage.

Tony had wrenched his back, but apparently this was related to an old injury, and one of the other monks knew how to treat it for him. He claimed he'd be fine once he got back to the monastery.

DeAndre had hit his head on a tree, and Tony thought the big man might have a concussion. DeAndre didn't believe it, though, and wouldn't hear of going to the hospital.

On a deeper level, Colin was the worst off. That burst of ki from Mrs. Tachibana hadn't just ripped through his wards. It had smacked him down hard on a spiritual level.

Still, Colin insisted he knew some healing magic from one of his books that would clear him up by morning. Or at least by the end of the weekend.

All, right, when pressed, he admitted he'd need about a week.

Tony and DeAndre, who'd been behind Tony's spiritual shield, had seemed to escape without any deeper harm, which Tony attributed to the Almighty.

He probably had a point. No doubt he'd been praying to Saint George for help against dragons.

Despite their protestations, the moment Nana Cyr came over she pushed remedies of her own on all three of them.

At least not one was foolish enough to try to say no.

While she did that, Heath took a moment to check on Nariko. He could tell that the burst of power she'd gotten earlier was fading, and she looked more than a little drained and pale.

"How are you?" he asked softly.

"Took some lumps," she said, just as quietly. "Mount Tabor healed the contusions for me, but babe, I'm *spent*. I need at least twelve hours sleep and one of your special omelets."

Heath quirked a grin at her. "You telling me you bluffed your mother?"

Nariko matched his smile. "*Maybe* I've picked up a trick or two, hanging out with you."

She gave him a quick kiss. Heath tried to ignore the coppery undertone.

"I don't do anything special to my omelets, you know," Heath said, frowning in puzzlement. "They're just food."

"My taste buds beg to differ," she said with a smile.

"Now that I don't think you'll bite my head off for saying so," Nana Cyr said, "you *need* to do something about all that blood."

Nana Cyr shoved a wet nap into Nariko's hand, making her laugh.

"I have some of those for leather cleaning in my car," DeAndre said in a tired voice. "Should help with your pants and my seats."

"Are you sure you're all right to drive, young man?" Nana Cyr asked DeAndre.

"No, ma'am," DeAndre said. "But my car can drive itself for me."

"Can *your* car do that?" Nana Cyr asked Heath.

Heath smiled and started to nod, but Nariko asked, "What car? You mean that trash pile Heath *calls* a car?"

"All right," Heath said, "if we've reached the point of mocking my ride, we can at least go get food."

"I need to get back," Tony said, audibly fighting down a groan.

"I can take him," DeAndre said.

"And *then* the hospital?" Nana Cyr asked, one eyebrow raised in judgment.

"Yes, ma'am," DeAndre said, as respectfully as Heath had ever heard him say anything. He sounded more normal, if wiped out, when he turned to Colin. "Can you get the rest home?"

Colin nodded, and led the way, pausing only so Nariko could clean her pants with DeAndre's leather wipes.

Before Heath put his grandmother in the front seat though — over her protests about his height and his need for the front seat — he gave her the biggest hug of thanks he'd given her in quite some time.

All she said in response then was the same thing she'd always said when he thanked her, as far back as he could remember.

"You're welcome, baby boy."

Something about the way she'd said it. As though the timing of her trip wasn't coincidental. As though she'd known he'd be in some kind of trouble that needed her help...

But then, that might have been exhaustion talking.

They were a quiet group in the car. Nariko dozed on Heath's shoulder, while he fired off a text message to Celia Martinez: "Found the person behind the gunman. Dealt with it. You three are clear."

Celia's response was immediate: "Good. Meet us at Gripper?"

"Not tonight," he sent back.

"You accused us by name. At Gripper. At least let us be seen drinking together tonight."

When Heath hesitated, Celia continued, "You owe us that much."

Heath sighed.

"Who are you texting?" Nariko mumbled.

"Tell you in a sec," Heath said, "Colin, would you drop me at Gripper?"

"Sure," Colin said, sounding puzzled. "What's up?"

Nariko made a sound of protest and snuggled in.

"I was overheard telling Maggie that Celia Martinez, Tommy Wong, and Stetson Price might have been behind the gunman. They want me to have a drink with them to show there's no bad blood."

Nariko growled, but moved away. "Home soon."

"I'll be as fast as I can." He told Celia he was on his way.

Nariko shoved her keys into Heath's hand. "Bring my bike home in one piece."

That was right. Her BMW motorcycle was still parked outside Gripper. He'd forgotten.

"Are you sure?" he asked. He knew how to ride, but he'd never ridden her bike without her before.

"In. One. Piece."

"All right, all right."

"Can I drop you at the corner of Burnside?" Colin asked. "I—"

"That's fine," Heath said, though his legs felt like they were groaning in protest. "It's only a half-block. What could go wrong?"

7

Colin dropped Heath right at the door of Gripper. Heath protested, but Colin refused to hear of doing otherwise. Even talked about not driving away until Heath was safely inside.

What could go wrong? What had Heath been thinking, daring the universe that way? Clearly he was even more exhausted than he'd realized.

Wasn't just Colin irritated with him either. The moment the words had left Heath's mouth, Nana Cyr had crossed herself, and made a gesture to ward off evil, just to be sure.

Even Nariko had given Heath a hard poke in the ribs.

Maybe the universe had decided Heath needed a break though. Or maybe Maggie had really lit into her grandmother, after Heath had left earlier. Because Mrs. Halloran let Heath inside without so much as a peep.

Gripper was jumping. Every table was filled with a diverse cross-section of the greater Portland occult community. Major and minor players, from a wide variety of practices and backgrounds.

Celia Martinez, Tommy Wong and Stetson Price were all waiting for Heath up at the bar, and they'd saved a stool for him. Tommy Wong was still in a dark suit, but he had on a red tie now. Stetson

Price had donned a silver shirt with what Heath thought of as cowboy lacing forming a pattern across it. Celia Martinez wore a bright red and yellow dress that made her look downright festive.

Maggie had a beer and a smile waiting for Heath by the time he reached the bar.

He had his drink. Made small talk about nothing. Clients (in general terms). Which herbs grew well around Portland, and which needed special care. Things he could talk about without giving them any information that anyone could call important or personal.

More than that, he refused movements into any topic that could be construed as indicating friendship.

He was willing to drink with them. Show there were no bad feelings. But he was *not* going to let them use this little display as anything they could spin into a show of support.

He specifically cut off any attempts to turn the subject to their "council" idea by shaking his head firmly and talking louder about nothing.

He could tell they were frustrated about this, but there wasn't much they could do about it.

When he finished his beer, he tried to pay for all their drinks, but Maggie just smiled wider and said, "Night's not done."

Just a little reminder that he was still on Mrs. Halloran's tab from earlier.

"Then let us buy *you* a drink," Stetson said, practically dripping with sincere hospitality.

"Can't," Heath said, fighting a yawn. "Gotta drive."

As Heath turned away, Maggie stopped him.

"Since you aren't sticking around," she said, "and since neither you nor your grandmother did much drinking in here…" She handed him a bottle of the bourbon Nana Cyr had been drinking earlier. Riverboat Bourbon, cask-aged twenty-two years, and worth quite a pretty penny. "Please present this to your grandmother with my compliments, and my hopes that I'll see her again before she returns to New York."

"Well," Heath said, drawing the word out. "I will be sure to pass all that along. And I think I'm safe thanking you on her behalf, and telling you she'll probably come by at least one more time before then."

"Please," Tommy Wong said, "present my compliments to your grandmother as well."

And then Celia Martinez and Stetson Price were saying it, and trying to use Nana Cyr as a conversational sally.

Heath didn't let them. He thanked them with a smile and turned away.

Mrs. Halloran didn't even say anything at the door. Just handed over his backpack without comment.

Heath thanked her anyway, and gave her a smile as he put that bottle of bourbon in his backpack before slinging it over his shoulder.

Soon as the door closed behind him, a limousine pulled up. The rear window buzzed down. Sitting inside was a man who didn't look old, but *elderly*. Italian, and from his skin tone, he might be the type who could trace his Italian heritage back to the Romans and beyond.

Thinning silver hair, but neatly combed straight back. He wore a tuxedo as though on his way to one of those big money charity events.

Even if power hadn't been rolling off the man in waves, Heath would have recognized him. He'd met him at crossed purposes when both had been working for Heath's landlord.

That man known as the Lammergeyer.

"Good evening, Mr. Cyr," he said in a cultured voice. "Might I offer you a lift?"

Heath shook his head. "Sorry. Have to get Nariko's bike back to her. Kind of you to offer though."

"And your refusal is most understandable," the Lammergeyer said without missing a beat. As though he'd expected the refusal, and only asked to see what reason he'd be given. "Would you be so kind then as to sit with me a moment?"

"I don't mean any offense," Heath said honestly, "but I've had a *long* day, and I just want to go home. Rain check?"

"Inadvisable," the Lammergeyer said, again without missing a beat. Heath was starting to get irritated by the man's unflappability. "The matter is somewhat time-sensitive."

Heath hesitated.

"I would regard it as a personal favor," the Lammergeyer said.

"Fine," Heath said with a sigh. A favor from the Lammergeyer was likely worth the effort. He nodded back toward Gripper. "Pretty tight in there, but I can probably find us a table."

"I've no doubt you could," the Lammergeyer said. "But this topic is ... not for other ears. Not yet."

He opened the door of the limo.

"You *must* be joking," Heath said. "I am *not* getting in that car."

"I swear on my power that if you sit with me, I will defend your safety of mind, body and soul with my life until such time as you willingly leave."

Heath gave the man a lopsided smile.

"Now, see, that's just a B-plus effort," Heath said. "For starters, how do I know you're even alive? Might be one of those European lich things. Or maybe even some ancient Egyptian mummy, hiding behind a veneer of Italian heritage. Wouldn't be the weirdest thing I've talked to this year."

The barest hint of a smile played about the Lammergeyer's lips and twinkled in his eye.

"Oh, but I could get to like you, Mr. Cyr." The Lammergeyer nodded. "Very well, how about this? I swear on my power that I will keep you safe — body, mind and soul — while we converse within my limousine."

Heath shook his head. "You make an offer, I decline, you say conversation over and *bam*. The world is short one Heath."

The Lammergeyer chuckled. "I should pay you to negotiate neutral ground meetings."

"My rates are reasonable," Heath said with a shrug.

"Enough levity. Heath Cyr, I swear by my power that if you agree to converse with me in my limousine, I shall guard your safety with all forces at my disposal until such time as you agree of your own will that the conversation is complete and we have gone our separate ways. Further, I swear by all spirits that aid me that neither I, nor any associated with me, bound by me, nor employed by me, will take any deleterious actions against you between the moment you agree and sunrise."

"Why sunrise?" Heath asked.

"I considered 'until you are again behind wards of your own making,' but decided you would interpret that as an excuse to follow you home. Sunrise seemed a reasonable compromise."

"Fair enough. I notice that you aren't asking for any constraints on *my* behavior."

"Call it a gesture of good will. You are, by reputation, not a man who *starts* fights, but a man who *ends* them."

"All right if the limo stays here? I don't want to walk back if I make you unhappy."

"Herbert will find parking close by."

"All right then," Heath said, hitching his backpack a little higher. "I formally agree to converse with you in your limousine under those terms."

The Lammergeyer slid over, and Heath got in.

THE LAMMERGEYER'S LIMOUSINE PRACTICALLY SMELLED LIKE MONEY. IT *did* smell like leather, but it didn't have a lot of choice in the matter. There was just too much leather to avoid it.

Soft leather, a dark red color, for the molded seats, heated against the evening chill. Both the set in back, where the Lammergeyer and Heath sat, and the matching seats facing them, which were empty.

The partition between the back and the driver's section was up, forming a solid black wall.

Heath briefly considered moving across, but decided it would look petty. As though he still didn't trust his host, even after all the promises.

Of course, Heath *didn't* trust the Lammergeyer. But still, no reason to *advertise* that.

Between sections of seats was a small bar, with a marble countertop. On it, a platter featuring array of high end cold cuts and cheeses. Also a cut crystal bottle of brown liquor, along with one crystal tumbler beside it.

The Lammergeyer held the match for the tumbler, and his contained about two fingers of what smelled like a very expensive honeyed scotch.

Heath almost smiled as he looked about. He'd thought the *Parakeet* was heavily enchanted. This limousine made Heath's Gremlin look like the heap of trash Nariko called it.

Damn near unassailable, this limo. And the driver ... Herbert? ... could probably handle a high speed chase without the Lammergeyer ever spilling a slice of cheese or a drop of scotch.

"Charcuterie?" the Lammergeyer offered, gesturing to the countertop. "Some scotch, perhaps?"

Heath's stomach reminded him it was empty. Still, he refused with a shake of his head. "Kind of you to offer, though."

The Lammergeyer nodded, as though he'd expected that reply.

But then the old man sighed.

"Mr. Cyr, you disappoint me."

"Yeah," Heath said, quirking an eyebrow. "That doesn't make you sound like a Bond villain at all."

Another twinkle around the eyes that seemed to be as close as the Lammergeyer came to smiling.

"The ways in which the Portland metro area would benefit from a council are countless, and extend well beyond the occult community itself."

Heath tried to fight the groan and lost.

"You?" he asked, incredulous. "You're the one behind this council nonsense?"

"I represent Vancouver. Did you expect Vancouver to forgo having a voice on the council?"

Vancouver, Washington. Just across the Columbia River from Portland.

"One, there is no council," Heath said, ticking points off on his fingers. "Two, there isn't going to *be* a council. And three, don't sit there and pretend this is some kind of gesture of civic duty."

"Whatever do you mean?"

Heath sighed. Shook his head.

"Look," he said, hoping those oaths really did bind this man and that Heath wasn't picking a fight when he was alone and not exactly at his best. "Everyone knows you run Vancouver. Maybe just the occult community, maybe not, but we all know you're in charge on that side of the river."

The Lammergeyer, at least, didn't try to deny it, so Heath continued.

"Taking over by force down here, now, that's a tough prospect. You'd have to deal with a lot of heavy hitters, and might lose your hold on Vancouver in the process."

The Lammergeyer steepled his fingers, but he didn't interrupt.

"So you sell some people on this council idea. If it fails, no loss. But if it flies, you get a seat. You're Vancouver, after all, and we all know it. Once you're there, well, you're a persuasive guy. Maybe you get the president role, or speaker, or whatever they call it. You get the top voice. From there, you probably have plans to handle the rest, and soon you're not just Vancouver, you're running the whole area."

"If people choose me for their leader, where is the harm?"

He sounded so damned reasonable it was all Heath could do not to reach out and slap him. But that would have been a colossally bad idea, and he knew it.

Hell, just talking as much as Heath had was a stupid idea. He was pretty sure of that. But he was tired enough his mouth just kept going.

"Lots of harm has been done by leaders the people chose. Don't make me start naming names."

"And you would put me in their company? Perhaps you should visit Vancouver before declaring such."

"I'm saying all kinds of people become bad leaders. Even those with the best goals. I like our community the way it is."

"Even though you had to come to a bar tonight when you are clearly drained near the point of collapse? Even though you had to make a public appearance tonight to avoid even the rumors of a problem between you and others?"

The Lammergeyer cocked an eyebrow.

"A council could handle disputes far more effectively. And could quash rumors—"

"More effectively? Maybe. More justly? I have my doubts. And *maybe* it could quash rumors — I don't call that a given — but it could also spread lies and disinformation."

"But—"

"Every person on any council is there because they have an agenda. Because there are things they want to change. I don't see any reason to make it easy for anyone to go on a power trip."

"Anyone?" the Lammergeyer said, raising one index finger the way some would raise an eyebrow. "Or me?"

"Anyone," Heath said with a shrug. "I don't have anything special against you."

"You harbor no ill will toward me over my role in the Saint Cyprian matter?"

"That was just business," Heath said.

"And what of the work of Flex? More business?"

Heath narrowed his eyes. "Shit. You own Flex, don't you? Maybe through shell companies or whatever, but it's yours."

The Lammergeyer did not so much as blink. Make a hell of a poker player that man, because he absolutely did not give anything away.

"Could I not just be interested in what one might call a comparable situation?"

"Look," Heath said, shaking his head and hefting his backpack. "Pretty sure we've gone as far as we can with this. You're not going to sell me on this council idea."

"Very well," the Lammergeyer said. "Thank you for your time and your honesty. I will not forget that I owe you a favor."

He held out a hand to shake. Heath had to remind himself of the man's promise.

Heath shook that hand. Cool skin, but a strong grip.

"Perhaps we can do business one day," the Lammergeyer said as Heath opened the door of the limousine. "I was serious about asking you to negotiate neutral ground arrangements."

"My rates are reasonable," Heath said, but smiled. "Considering the quality of the service."

The Lammergeyer chuckled appreciatively.

Heath stepped out into the night.

Heath might not have trusted the Lammergeyer, but the old man was true to his word about at least this much — when Heath got out of the limousine, he wasn't more than ten steps away from Nariko's motorcycle and his own parked car.

Had to be close to midnight as that limo pulled away. The night air felt pleasantly crisp. The interior of the limo must have been warmer than Heath had realized. Or maybe that was just the heated seat.

Heath stood on the asphalt beside that silver BMW and thought about the things he should do.

His own car could wait until tomorrow. Charmed as it was, no one would bother it overnight.

As for the motorcycle, he knew he should lay a trick to keep anyone from following him home. Just sound policy with some kind of politics brewing about.

He knew he should probably even take a couple of extra protective steps as well. Little bit of juju to keep any threats at bay.

But he was just too damned tired.

"Papa Legba," he whispered, pulling his silver flask out of his backpack. "Keep an eye on this little fool and make sure he gets home in one piece."

He poured out a little of his special rum for Papa Legba.

He repeated his prayer two more times, pouring out a little more rum each time as an offering.

He put the flask away and fired off a quick text message to Nariko, Colin, and Tony about the conversation he'd just had. Then, for good measure, he forwarded that text to Maggie.

Better that she knew sooner than later about this council business, and Heath had never promised discretion.

He put his hand on the tank of Nariko's BMW.

"Hey there," he said to the spirit of the bike. He may not have understood the way she'd enchanted the motorcycle, but spirits were something that made sense to him. "Know you remember me. Just want to take you home to Nariko, all right? She asked me to do it, and she's waiting at my place."

Heath mounted up and started the bike.

It took off before he even tried the accelerator.

All he could do was hold on for dear life as the BMW rocketed through the streets of Portland all the way to his neighborhood, up his driveway, and screeched to a stop just shy of his porch.

It all happened so fast that Heath could only sit there in shock.

Nariko opened the door. Didn't look like she was wearing anything but his shirt again. That green and white striped one from earlier. Her hair was all tousled, and her eyes were full of sleep.

"Bed," she said.

"Nari," Heath said, shaking himself and dismounting the bike before it did something even crazier, like try to bite him. "Your bike—"

"Did what it had to do." She nodded. "Bed *now*."

"Right," Heath said, trotting up onto his porch and into her arms.

Nariko lay her head against his chest as though she'd go to sleep standing there.

"Nari," he whispered. "Bed is that way."

"Comfy," she said.

He smiled and shook his head. He scooped her up in his arms, and she nestled in with a happy sigh.

He closed the door with his foot. A glance told him his grandmother was already asleep on the lounge chair in his living room.

Good.

"Don't want a snack?" he asked.

"Later," Nariko mumbled. "Bed now."

He carried her down the hall.

"Nari," he whispered. "You know, we can't just stay in bed the next few days. Nana's here, and I need to show her Portland. Plus, we owe Tony, Colin and DeAndre a pretty darn good dinner. At least."

Nariko hmphed. "Owe me."

"And I plan to make good on it, believe me," Heath said. "Also, Nana Cyr wants me to buy a proper suit."

"Mmmm," she said, smiling. "Dress you up nice. Sounds fun."

As Heath entered his bedroom, he smiled again at the sight of a very sleepy Dr. John waiting among the rumpled sheets of his bed.

Dr. John looked up and mewed as though he, like Nariko, was irritated that Heath was not yet naked and in bed.

And to be honest, Heath was a little irritated about that too.

So he kicked the bedroom door closed behind him, and he took Nariko to bed.

SIGN UP FOR STEFON'S NEWSLETTER

Stefon loves to keep in touch with his readers, and loves to keep you reading. The best way for him to do both is for you to sign up for his newsletter.

Sign up at http://www.stefonmears.com/join

If you sign up for Stefon's newsletter, you get...

- Monthly updates about his publishing and travel schedules
- His latest news, in brief, and answers to reader questions
- A free short story for signing up
- List-only offers and occasional specials
- Plus a free short story every month!

ABOUT THE AUTHOR

Stefon Mears would love to check out the Set Piece Brewpub. Stefon has more than thirty books to his credit, and he never stops writing. He earned his M.F.A. in Creative Writing from N.I.L.A., and his B.A. in Religious Studies (double emphasis in Ritual and Mythology) from U.C. Berkeley. He's a lifelong gamer and fantasy fan. Stefon lives in Portland, Oregon, with his wife and three cats.

Look for Stefon online:
www.stefonmears.com
himself@stefonmears.com